GAMES

GAMES

by Bill Pronzini

G. P. Putnam's Sons, New York

SBN: 399-11588-9
Library of Congress Catalog Card Number: 76-25413

PRINTED IN THE UNITED STATES OF AMERICA

For the memory of my father,
Joseph Pronzini
(1908–1973)

GAMES

PROLOGUE

Friday, May 8: WASHINGTON

One must test oneself to see if one is meant for independence and for command. And one must do it at the right time. Never avoid your tests, though they may be the most dangerous game you can play, and in the end are merely tests at which you are the only witness and the sole judge.

—NIETZSCHE, *Beyond Good and Evil*

IN THE PRIVATE OFFICE of his suite on Capitol Hill, Senator David Jackman sat brooding out the window adjacent to his desk, elbows resting on the padded arms of his chair, fingers laced under his chin. A light rain pattered softly against the glass, slid down it in intricate configurations. The rain had been falling steadily for five days now, and it was beginning to depress him; Washington under wet skies was the grayest place in the world.

He swiveled abruptly to the desk, and his gaze moved in a restless turn around the office. Heavy, dark wood paneling and furnishings. Old-burgundy carpet. Bookshelves floor to ceiling on two walls. Subdued lighting, an absence of bright color. The overall effect was one of pure functionalism: no frills of any kind. On days such as this, however, it also developed an aura of mustiness, of almost Victorian austerity, like something out of Dickens.

His eyes lowered to the desktop and then held on the two framed photographs arranged side by side on the polished surface: one of Meg, taken ten years ago when there had been no artifice in her smile, no cupidity behind the guileless brown eyes; one of himself and the Old Man, taken in 1966 on the island.

It was amazing how much he looked like the Old Man, Jackman thought. Same long, broad, ascetic face. Same carefully brushed, carefully trimmed black hair. Same intelligent, alert expression and strong jaw and gleaming white teeth. Two generations of clean-cut, all-American men; good men, perhaps even great men, bearing the weight of public office on their squared shoulders, standing tall and indomitable and forever prepared to fight with unselfish zeal for the vital needs and causes of the country, of the world.

Bullshit, he thought.

And even though he did not turn his head, he was aware in that moment of the two dozen black-and-white film stills on the wall behind him. *I, Camera, Eye:* an artistic, impressionistic slice of life seen from the interchanging points of view of a man and a camera, the man as a camera, the camera as a sentient eye. He had written it, directed it, and coproduced it with three friends in college in the late fifties, and it had won honorable mention at Cannes and been favorably received at the New York and San Francisco film festivals. The critics had said it showed great promise; the critics had said they were eager to see his next film. Only there had not been a next film. The Old Man had seen to that.

And here I am, he thought. For better and for worse, a mediocre and slightly tarnished, if conscientious, champion of the people. *I, Senator, Aye.*

He massaged his temples: his head ached dully. Christ, it had been a long day. Morning meeting of the D.C. Committee, at which two representatives of the NAACP had demanded that something be done about the severe underrepresentation of blacks on the Washington police force. Lunch with two Maine congressmen to discuss reforestation policies. A quorum call this afternoon for the military aid to Lebanon bill, and then a conference with two of his aides who were trying to convince him to attend a campaign-deficit dinner in California next month. Smile and agree, smile and disagree; silence when necessary, eloquence when necessary. Honest manipulation, forthright maneuvering. Move and countermove.

It's all a game, David, never forget that. Life, love, politics—just games. Once you learn how to play them, once you become an accomplished gamesman, you'll never have to look up at any man or back on any decision.

If he concentrated Jackman could hear, echoing in the dim corners of memory, the Old Man's voice saying those words a quarter of a century ago. Those words, and others like them. The Philosophy of Thomas R. Jackman, United States Senator and Unsuccessful Aspirant for the Presidency, Now Deceased. Maybe I ought to have that philosophy engraved on a plaque that I can hang in here next to my law degree, he thought, not for the first time and not frivolously.

Because the thing was, the Old Man had spoken the truth. Which was ironic when you considered that he had spent his career in the Senate bending and reshaping truth and honor to his own ends, making up his own rules for the games he played. Jackman recalled the Wendell Phillips quote again: "You can always get the truth from an American statesman after he has turned seventy, or given up all hope for the Presidency." Except that Thomas R. Jackman had died of a heart attack at the age of sixty-four, while engaged in yet another futile drive for a presidential nomination.

Still, the philosophy itself was basically valid. Everything *was* a game; you could translate any situation, any goal, any facet of life, into those terms. Play the games well and you were a winner; play them poorly and you were a loser. Simple as that. And Jackman had learned to play them well, all right—learned the intricacies and the strategies and the nuances. The only difference between him and his father was that he played by constitutional and lawful and mostly ethical rules rather than by rules he and he alone devised. Even his opponents in and out of politics, men like James Turner and

Alan Pennix who bitterly refuted his liberal policies and spoke out against the "Jackman family dynasty," had not been able to label him a total simulacrum of his father. . . .

The intercom burred: his secretary, Miss Bigelow. Loyal and competent, Bigelow, if not much in the way of window dressing; she was fifty-four, going to fat in the middle and hips, and had a pronounced mustache because she had stopped using depilatories when she reached the five-decade mark. He had inherited her from the Old Man, for whom she had worked during the fifteen years prior to his death: she was a team player all the way.

"Yes?"

"Your wife called, Senator."

"Called? She didn't ask to speak with me?"

"No sir, she said it wasn't necessary. She left a message."

"All right."

"She's decided to attend the Women's Caucus benefit tonight," Miss Bigelow said. "She expects to be home rather late."

"I see. Was that all?"

"No. She asked that I tell you she made airline reservations for Boston this afternoon. United Flight Fifteen, leaving May twenty-first at seven-thirty P.M. You're to call her father if you feel you can get away."

Memorial Day weekend near Boston, with Meg's stuffy family on their stuffy estate. Or was that really where she was going? She knew he had no intention of joining her there; he had made that clear to her when they discussed the subject earlier in the week. Meg was very good at game-playing too, which was one of the reasons why he had been attracted to her in the beginning.

"Fine," he said. "Thank you, Elaine."

He sat for a moment and then swiveled his chair again and looked at the window, watched the rain stream down the pane, the grayness beyond. Memorial Day weekend. Three long days, free days, because he had no pressing engagements. And he thought about sun, and about the smell of pines and the smell of the sea, and about the summers of his youth.

He thought about the island.

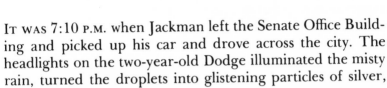

It was 7:10 p.m. when Jackman left the Senate Office Building and picked up his car and drove across the city. The headlights on the two-year-old Dodge illuminated the misty rain, turned the droplets into glistening particles of silver, reflected blurrily off the wet street.

After twenty-five minutes he slowed at an intersection, swung into another street, and drifted in to the curb in front of the third building on the right side of the block. This was one of Washington's better neighborhoods, quiet and expensive, not far from the Potomac; the building was ivied, and there was an arched front door and round-topped windows and hanging carriage lamps—not unlike the house in which he and Meg lived in Georgetown. Add a sycamore here, a Dutch elm there, a decorative fountain in the center of a curving front drive, and he might have been coming home.

Might have been. Coming home.

He shut off the engine, the headlights, and got out into the drizzle and locked the doors and then ran up onto the colonnaded porch. There were two flats in the building; he rang the bell for the top one. A moment later the door buzzed softly, and he went inside and climbed the stairs two at a time.

Tracy was there and waiting for him, as Meg so seldom had been these past few years.

13

LIKE EVERYTHING ELSE, sex was a game. When two people played it well together, it was very good; and ·he aftermath was warm and filled with sweet fragrances and a kind of luxuriant repose. It had been that way with Meg at first, but not anymore; she played the sex game, at least with him, out of necessity rather than pleasure, duty rather than love or affection. Not so Tracy. Tracy took as much joy in giving as in receiving, and her enthusiasm and her inventiveness were boundless. You could immerse yourself in her. In Meg, you could only float emptily on the surface of feeling.

They lay quiescent in Tracy's bed, her head cradled against his chest, and he stroked her hair gently with the tips of his fingers. The room was feminine, but without coyness, and tastefully decorated in lavenders and whites. The only light came from a small, low-wattage bedside lamp.

After a while he said, "I've been thinking."

"That's good."

"Specifically, I mean, about Memorial Day weekend. I'd like to get away for it—a short vacation. I haven't had even that for months now. Senators should have vacations every now and then, don't you think?"

"Absolutely," Tracy said. "They absolutely should."

"How would you like to join me?"

"I'd like that very much. Can we arrange it?"

"We can."

"Did you have some place particular in mind?"

"Particular, and private. A private island."

"I didn't know there were such things anymore."

"There are lots of them off the north coast of Maine," Jackman said. "I seem to have co-inherited one, as a matter of fact."

14

She leaned up on one elbow so that she could look down into his face. "Are you serious, David?"

"Politicians are always serious."

"I didn't know you had an island."

"I don't advertise the fact."

"What sort of island is it?"

"Oh, not much as islands go. About three square miles, covered mostly by pine and spruce forest. My father bought it in the thirties and built a summer home on it; I spent most of my boyhood summers there. I haven't gone much since he died. Meg doesn't like islands."

"I love islands," Tracy said.

"So do I. We'll love it together Memorial Day weekend."

"It occurs to me that you must have someone living there the year round. You'd hardly leave a summer home unattended on a private island."

"There's a caretaker—the same one my father hired in 1937."

A puckish smile. "And he approves of you bringing your mistresses up for weekends?"

"You make it sound as if I've had a string a mile long."

"Haven't you?"

"No," he said seriously, and thought but did not say: There has only been you and a girl named Alicia, only two. "What I usually do is to wire a message to him in Weymouth Village a few days ahead and let him know I'm coming—"

"*Wire* a message?"

"There aren't any telephones on the island."

"How come?"

"Too far out from the mainland, for one thing. For another, my father didn't care to have his summers cluttered up with a lot of unimportant political and private business. Messages, important or otherwise, have always been taken out by boat from the village."

"Wow—the nineteenth century still lives."

"You won't think so after you've seen the house," he said. "Anyhow, if I tell the caretaker, Jonas, that I don't want to be

15

disturbed, he'll take the family boat in to Weymouth and leave it in a boathouse we rent there. When I leave we reverse the procedure. Generally I look him up to say hello, but he won't think anything of it if I don't."

"So we'll be completely alone together."

"Just us, and the seabirds and the little beasties that live in the piny woods."

"It sounds idyllic."

"It is. Settled, then?"

"What about your wife?"

Liberated woman, Tracy: direct, frank, no mincing of words. Not at all like Meg, who played all of her games by circumlocution and euphemism. Jackman liked directness, had always liked it. Tracy was the kind of woman, in fact, that had appealed to him strongly since puberty; strange, then, now that he considered it, that he should have married someone like Meg. And why *had* he married Meg? They had had game-playing in common, but little else; and the love he had thought was binding had turned out to be weak and tenuous. They had grown in opposite directions, grown out of love and into an arrangement: no divorce by mutual consent, because it might harm both their images; elaborate pretenses at public and family functions and at media interviews; lovers acceptable by tacit agreement, just so long as the affairs were carried on with the utmost discretion. It was probably a good thing, he thought, that she had been born with a tipped uterus. Children would not have cemented their marriage, and children do not flourish in an arrangement. . . .

"David?"

"Sorry," he said. "I was woolgathering. Don't worry about Meg; she's going to spend Memorial Day with her family in Boston. Or so she says."

"Then it's settled. When do we leave?"

"Friday the twenty-second, early morning?"

"Beautiful."

"We'll take separate seats on a flight to Bangor," he said.

16

"Then we'll rent a car, or you will, and we'll drive up the coast—"

He stopped, because in that moment, with sudden objectivity, he saw and heard himself: United States Senator David Jackman, friend of the people, hater of political chicanery, deeply involved in just causes, lying naked in the bed and arms of a woman who was not his wife and planning a furtive weekend. God! It might have been funny in an ironic sense, like JFK's amorous adventures, but he could not seem to rationalize it that way. Not funny—pathetic, a little disgusting.

And then he thought: For Christ's sake, it's just a game—and the moment passed. Just a game: not one he wanted to play, one he was *forced* to play. Nothing to do with politics, that was a different game entirely. You had to play thousands of games during the course of a lifetime, and if one of them was less than moral or honorable, it could be forgiven, it did not have to affect the individual as a whole.

Tracy seemed to think he had finished naturally. She said, "And we'll spend the entire weekend balling, maybe even out among those beasties in the piny woods."

She sounded pleased and excited, and he told himself he felt the same way; in her arms he had lost the depression caused by the rain, and now he had the weekend, and Tracy, and the island to look forward to. "Yes," he said. "Anywhere you want, Ty. Anytime."

But when she laughed and said "How about again right now?" and drew his head to her breasts, the only real anticipation in him was for the island itself; and he had, inexplicably, the same vague kind of lost and lonely feeling he had experienced sometimes as a child.

17

PART ONE

Friday, May 22:
THE ISLAND

*There is the isle of tombs, the silent isle; there too are the tombs of my youth.
There I wish to carry an evergreen wreath of life.*

—NIETZSCHE, "The Tomb Song," *Thus Spake Zarathustra*

OVER THE HAMMERING pulse of the boat engine, Jackman said, "There it is, dead ahead."

From this distance the island appeared long and flattened down, fitted to the juncture of bright blue water and pale blue sky; the gradual hump to the right of center was ascendant forestland and the jagged line of cliffs which rose a hundred feet above sea level and formed part of the southern, seaward shore. Oblong in shape, as were most of these Maine coastal islands, it ran two miles northeast-southwest and slightly more than a mile northwest-southeast. The pine and spruce woods covering roughly three-quarters of its surface were a brownish-green smear through the late-afternoon haze.

Beside him at the wheel, Tracy leaned forward with her hands on top of the open windscreen. "How far away is it, David?"

"More than a mile." *Watch it grow, boy,* the Old Man had told him at the beginning of one of those long-ago childhood summers. *It grows right before your eyes.* "Watch it grow," Jackman said to her.

21

Except for the plumelike fan of the cruiser's wake, the surface of the sea was flat and unruffled; the day was unseasonably warm, temperature in the high seventies, windless. The smell of salt was so sharp that you felt as though you could taste it. Gulls wheeled in lazy circles overhead, but nothing else moved, no other boat.

The cruiser—a nineteen-foot Chris-Craft, mahogany finish and brightwork gleaming in the sun—planed smoothly past two bare-rock islets and drew abeam of another, wooded one to starboard. This area of the coast, north of Bar Harbor, was a bay of islands—more like a lake district, with its calm waters and archipelagic acres of woods and meadowland, than a part of the Atlantic Ocean. Jackman Island, nine and a half miles from the mainland, was farther out and somewhat more isolated than most.

The coastline itself was a complex labyrinth of bays and headlands, and the drive from Bangor, once they had left State Route 1, had taken them alongside and across saltwater inlets and marshes, bridges and causeways, peninsulas and inshore islands. Jackman remembered the drive with pleasure: sun and shadow, sea and sky, the cool salt breeze and the cries of gulls and great blue herons. All such a long, long way from Washington.

They had gotten to Weymouth Village shortly past three o'clock. Jackman had not been there in nearly two years, but it hadn't changed any in that time; it hadn't really changed any that he could recall since his first summer visit at the age of nine—aloof from progress, unspoiled by tourism. The nineteenth-century church and schoolhouse, the birdlimed Civil War monument in the village green, the line of old white houses ringing the narrow harbor, the clustered masts of the lobster boats bows-on to the tide, and the grizzled men who owned them grouped along the wharf to take in the sun: peaceful, what had once been called quaint before that word became overused. The Jackman family boathouse was on the northeastern side of the harbor, and the Chris-Craft had been locked inside when he and Tracy got there. Jonas, the

22

caretaker, had not been around, nor had anyone else. Wearing sunglasses and the brand-new sports outfit, complete with canvas shoes and a jaunty sailor's cap, which Tracy had presented to him as a "weekend gift" the night before, Jackman had felt both a little foolish and a little furtive—the first attack of conscience he had suffered since the one in Tracy's flat two weeks ago.

As the boat drew closer, now, the island took on familiar contours: the cobble beaches and mudflats of the sheltered north shore, visible because the tide was at ebb; the dense pine and spruce forest, studded here and there with oak and white birch; the rocky cliffs and headlands, wet with spray from the open sea; off the southwest shore, the four tiny satellite islands, only one of which was large enough to support vegetation. The summerhouse and the wide bay, which it overlooked on the northwest shore, were still hidden by trees and by the long arm of land the Old Man had christened Eider Neck in honor of the ducks that nested there.

Approaching the island again after two years, Jackman found himself pervaded with nostalgia and a sense of well-being, and he wondered why he had denied this to himself for so long. It was the one place he felt truly at home, the one place he knew better than any other, and loved, and could become one with. Meg hated it because of its isolation, its primitive nature—the precise reasons why it attracted him. Opposites in every meaningful way, it seemed, he and Meg. Opponents. He would have found time to come to the island often if she had shared his feelings; as it was, he should have found time to come alone.

"Where do we land?" Tracy asked. "That shore looks pretty rocky."

"There's a bay around that arm of land there on our left, Eider Neck. It's one of only two places you can put a boat in to the island; the other one is around on the east shore. There are ledges jumbled everywhere else. You can see some of them when we get closer: it's low tide."

"Is that where the house is, at the bay?"

23

"Yes."

Jackman cut the wheel to port, to make the loop around the rock- and meadow-carpeted hump of Eider Neck. There was still no other craft in the vicinity, and the aura of vast sun-swept emptiness, of being utterly alone, was enormous; and yet, there was no loneliness in it. Out here, Jackman had never felt alone in any way.

The long ragged sweep of the headland on the far side of the bay came into view as they neared the tip of the Neck, running at right angles to it several hundred yards offshore to avoid the ledges and the uncovered mudflats. The rich resin scent of the evergreens carried to him on the warm air—a sweet fragrance like that of Tracy, or Meg in the early years, after they had finished making love. Jackman's throat felt curiously dry.

Then he could see the bay, and the boathouse at the end of the wooden dock, and the three white buildings set on high ground two hundred yards inland from the half-moon, shale-and-cobblestone beach. A clipped, sloping lawn stretched between the house and the beach, dotted with ornate black-iron poles on which carriage-style lanterns had been hung in the old days; they resembled, at least to Jackman's mind, uniform pieces scattered on a bright green gameboard. Pine and spruce made a dark green backdrop to the northeast, east and south. Cleared paths, two of several on the island, wound upward and away through the trees on both inner sides of the cove.

The Old Man had modeled the summerhouse after post-Revolution Maine cottages, only double the normal size because that was the way he had always done things. It had sixteen rooms, four fireplaces, a sharp-pitched roof, narrow oblong windows—but he had spoiled the replica by adding a wide, pillared veranda onto the whole of the front. The much smaller swelling a hundred yards to the north and fifty yards below the main house was of a simple frame type, built on a fieldstone foundation; this was where Jonas lived with

24

his wife. The other building, behind and to the southeast of the house, was a combination woodshed and storage barn.

Jackman took the boat carefully into the bay, cutting power, and angled it across toward the boathouse. The wide entrance doors were latched open. When he maneuvered the Chris-Craft inside, Tracy, good sailor, jumped onto the narrow platform along the left-hand wall and made the bowline fast. He shut down the engine, swung their bags onto the walk, tied the stern line, and moved back to pull the doors closed with a long hooked pole kept there for that purpose. Then they went out onto and along the dock, Jackman portering.

"That's quite a summerhouse," Tracy said. "It looks big enough to subdivide."

"My father liked a lot of room and a lot of people around, even in the summer," Jackman said. "We always had house guests, and two or three parties a week. Catered, for God's sake."

"The good old carefree days."

"For me, maybe, growing up. Not for the world at large; we were at war part of that time." The Old Man fiddling while the whole world damned near burned, he thought. Liquor flowing while blood flowed on alien soil; mourning in radio speeches the American loss of life on Guam and Leyte and the beaches at Anzio, with a Maine suntan and a voice made husky by too many gin rickeys and too much island laughter. And I wonder what would have happened to this country if Thomas R. Jackman had succeeded in his ambition to become President?

They came down off the dock and onto the path that skirted the rim of the beach. Seaweed and driftwood lay over and among the rocks, deposited by high tides; the remains of two dead flounder added a faint stench of decay to the salt-and-evergreen scent. When they were opposite the house, Jackman led the way off the path and across the lawn and up onto the veranda.

The front door opened into a large foyer: an antique table and a gilt-framed mirror, a pegged coatrack in lieu of a closet, the staircase to the upper floor. To the right was a wide archway, and they went through there and into the parlor. This room was large enough to sit and stand thirty people comfortably; it had paneled walls and pine flooring, leather furniture, brass accessories, heavy wool-twist rugs, an antique grandfather's clock, a standing leather-fronted bar in the far corner. A native-stone fireplace covered most of the inner wall lengthwise.

He put their bags down beside the couch and then stood still for a moment. In his mind he could hear the ghostly echo of voices and clinking glasses and the muted strains of "Over the Rainbow" and "Twilight Time" as they had been played by the three-piece band the Old Man had hired out of Milbridge. Empty and immaculate, the room felt incomplete. An atmosphere of waiting seemed to linger within it, as if it needed people, gaiety, life, to give it a life of its own.

But the old days were dead and gone, buried along with the Old Man and with his submissive and perpetually smiling wife, who had preceded him to the grave by six years. Jackman's older brother, Dale, a New York cliff dweller who had forsaken politics for the parallel game of Big Business, brought his wife and family here for the month of July every year; and Jackman himself had come exactly five times since the Old Man's fatal heart attack eight years before. Aside from these visits, and aside from periodic dustings by Jonas' wife, the house stood deserted and alone: watching the seasons come and the seasons go. . . .

He asked Tracy, "What do you think so far?"

"Impressive. When do the caterers arrive for us?"

He laughed. "Drink first, or the grand tour?"

"How about both? I'm thirsty *and* curious."

"Fair enough. Old-fashioned?"

"No, liberated." Standard joke between them.

Jackman went behind the bar—well-stocked as always,

plenty of fresh ice in the portable icemaker—and made an old-fashioned for Tracy and a rum tonic for himself. Then, carrying their drinks, they went up the staircase to the second floor.

Two guest bedrooms, each with a private bath. Servants' quarters. Storage room. Master bedroom: canopied four-poster his mother had bought in a shop in Bar Harbor and which the Old Man had said was "too damned flimsy for a marital couch"; white rugs on the floor, white lace curtains. She had made this room her own, if none other in the house and little else in her married life.

Standing in the doorway, Tracy said, "God, it looks bloody virginal. We're not going to sleep here, are we?"

Jackman gave her an uncomfortable glance. Showing her these upstairs rooms, he had developed a vague feeling of guilt, as though he were committing a sacrilege by bringing a woman who was not his wife into the house—as though the house itself realized this, and disapproved, and transmitted that disapproval to him by osmosis. What would the Old Man have said about Tracy? Well, the Old Man had not exactly been a paragon of fidelity, if you could believe the rumors about him—and you almost certainly could. So he would probably have smiled in his sly way, given a knowing wink, and: *Just another game, David, a harmless diversion. Play and enjoy. But be careful of your moves. . . .*

"No," Jackman said. "Not here. We'll use one of the guest rooms, the biggest one down at the end of the hall."

He took her into Dale's room. Walls covered with Harvard pennants, the model ship he had built one summer still sitting in the middle of the writing desk. Then, finally, they entered Jackman's boyhood room. Familiar view of the bay and Eider Neck and the island-dotted waters beyond, books placed neatly on the shelves against one wall: biographies of historical figures, volumes dealing with cinematography and film technique, adventure and classic novels, the collected works of Lewis Carroll bound in worn leather. Everything

27

just as it had always been, because neither he nor Dale had wanted it changed. The memories of this place were too good and too perfect to want for alteration of any kind.

Tracy picked out one of the leather tomes. "I didn't know you were into Lewis Carroll."

"Pretty heavily a long time ago," he said, and smiled, and felt himself relaxing again. "'Twas brillig, and the slithy toves/ Did gyre and gimbel in the wabe;/All mimsy were the borogoves'—"

"—'And the mome raths outgrabe,'" she said. "I was weaned on 'Jabberwocky.'"

"Can you still recite the whole poem?"

"I think so. Can you?"

"Well let's see. . . . "

He began to quote as they went out into the hall again, and Tracy joined in, and the only line they stumbled over was "Long time the manxome foe he sought—" By the time they were finished, he had taken her through the library downstairs—hundreds of books, all of them law texts or political treatises; no fiction because the Old Man had been too unimaginative and too much of a plotter himself to take pleasure from the mind games of others—and then into the study.

This had been Thomas Jackman's retreat, and it was a completely masculine but somehow cold and impersonal room, as if it had been contrived to fit an image rather than suited naturally to a man's personality. Deep leather chairs, hunting prints, primitive art, the traditional stag's head mounted on the wall over the massive oak desk, the—

Jackman stopped five paces into the room, frowning. "Now that's odd," he said.

"What is?"

He pointed across to the free-standing, glass-door cabinet opposite the desk. The doors were open wide, and the cabinet was empty. "My father kept his collection of guns in there," he said. "Half a dozen rifles—he had deer brought to the island when he bought it—and twenty or so handguns."

28

"Well maybe the caretaker took them out to clean them, or whatever else it is you do with guns."

"I suppose so."

But he was thinking that Jonas was a fussy sort and so was his wife. He couldn't imagine either of them leaving the doors standing open like that. And there were gun oil and rags and such in the drawer at the bottom of the cabinet; Jonas wouldn't have had any reason that Jackman could see to take the weapons to his own house, or away with him to the mainland.

Someone else—an intruder?

No, of course not. Jonas never allowed visitors without direct permission, and he invariably made the rounds before he left the island. He wouldn't have left at all if there had been trespassers or indications of trespassers. Still, someone *could* have landed a boat illegally at the cove on the east shore, after Jonas and his wife had gone. . . .

Well Christ, Jackman thought, there hadn't been any sign of forcible entry and nothing else was missing or out of place in the house. Prowlers would have taken other things besides the guns; there were at least a dozen items more valuable on the premises. For whatever reason, Jonas had removed the guns from the cabinet, no one else.

Tracy was looking at him. "You don't think anything's wrong, do you?"

"No, of course not." He pushed the missing guns from his mind and put his arm around her shoulders. "Come on," he said, "you haven't seen the room where you'll be spending most of your time."

"What room is that?"

"The kitchen, where else?"

She gave him a sweet smile. "Fuck you, Senator," she said.

THEY HAD SECOND DRINKS on the veranda, sitting in wicker armchairs and looking out over the bay. It was almost five-thirty now, and the sun had drifted low in the west; the sky had a glazed, coppery look. There was a stirring of wind, edged with coolness, and later, during the night and early morning, Jackman knew there would be one of the summer mists he had watched fascinated from his bedroom window as a boy. *And a grey mist on the sea's face and a grey dawn breaking.* Masefield? Yes: *I must down to the seas again, to the lonely sea and the sky.* . . .

Tracy said, "Is it always this still here? If it wasn't for a gull once in a while, there wouldn't be any sound at all."

"Usually, in weather like this."

"It's kind of eerie. I feel as though I'm somewhere at the end of the world."

"You'll get used to it soon enough," he said. "It's the most tranquil place on earth."

"I hope so. Right now I feel more edgy than tranquil."

He looked at her beside him, in profile, and thought again—exactly as he had the first time he'd seen her—that she possessed an almost classic beauty. Every feature flawless: full-lipped mouth, slightly rounded chin, Grecian nose, high cheekbones, silky complexion, thick-lashed hazel eyes that would turn a bright glittery green with passion or intense emotion. Midnight-black hair, worn long and flowing; immaculately proportioned body; unaffected grace in each movement. A fascinating woman, Tracy Haddon. And an enigmatic one.

In the ten months Jackman had known her, he had never been able to fathom the depths of her personality. She was a complex individual, fashioned of anomalies; a private person who offered no explanations and no excuses for what she was

30

and what she did. She had a BA in history from the University of Virginia, and yet she had made a successful career for herself as a writer of film documentaries. She was a self-admitted feminist, and yet she had taken and seemed to relish an almost totally submissive role in their affair. She had said on one occasion that the lust for wealth was the greatest of all sins, and on another occasion that if money couldn't buy happiness, it could buy something very close to it. She hated deception of all types, but she took a kind of perverse pleasure in the machinations necessary to keep their relationship a secret. She thought politics was "ridden with corrupt fools, bullshit artists, and hamstrung martyrs," that it was ultimately a futile and frustrating exercise for the average citizen to become involved, and yet she had chosen to work with and among politicos in the Washington milieu: the bulk of the documentaries she wrote were concerned with political life or figures.

It was just such a documentary, for PBS, which had brought about their meeting. He was in the early stages of his first campaign for reelection, and the subject of the film was just such a campaign: a study of freshmen senators and congressmen and their feelings about reelection, why they had chosen to run again, what they felt they had accomplished in their first term, and what they hoped to accomplish if there was a second—that kind of thing. She had been one of the group who had approached him, had been present at each of a series of taped interviews; had spent a good deal of time with him, off and on, in Washington and in Bangor, until just a few days before the election itself (which he had won in a landslide; the Jackmans always won in Maine and always in landslides).

He had been mildly infatuated from the first, by her beauty and by her involvement in filmmaking: she was doing the kind of thing he had always wanted to do himself, would have done himself if it had not been for the Old Man. She had been impressed when he told her about *I, Camera, Eye*, and they had discussed film and film theory whenever the

31

opportunity presented itself. But it had been too soon after the difficult affair with Alicia, and he had been too committed to his campaign and to his work in the Senate to make or even seriously consider advances. And her own attitude toward him had been one of interest in the senator but apparent indifference toward the man. Or so he had thought. She told him later that she had felt a growing attraction from the beginning, but that she had kept it hidden because she was not the kind of woman who got off on going to bed with a public figure, and because he had never given any indication of being open to a relationship.

Perhaps their affair would never have begun if it had not been for a chain of circumstances. His election victory, and Tracy being out of Washington when he returned there from Bangor. The bitter fight he had had with Meg two days later, over the quite minor question of redecorating their house in Georgetown. The fact that he had decided to work late at his office that same night, after Miss Bigelow and the rest of his staff had left, rather than go home to a continuation of the battle with Meg. The fact that Tracy had come in on a night flight from New York and had called from the airport with the intention of leaving a message on his answering machine that her company wanted to arrange a final interview for the documentary. The conversation they'd had, innocent enough but leading to an impulsive invitation to her to stop up on her way home to discuss that final interview. The look of her when she arrived, and the two drinks they had shared, and the easy rapport between them, and the quiet emptiness of the office, and the developing aura of intimacy, and the long and sudden moment of silence in which they seemed to realize mutual willingness and mutual need. And then the first kiss, and the sharp urgency, and Jackman hearing himself say "I want you, I can't help it," and Tracy saying "Yes, right here, right *now*," with her eyes shining green and shameless, and the tearing away of clothing as they sank to the soft carpet, and the feel of her naked body, and the column of her arched neck, and the soft wetness of her, and the orgasms, and the holding, and the admixture of guilt and excitement he had felt at the commencement of a brand-new game.

That night had always seemed vaguely surreal in retrospect, a kind of sensual fantasy trip. On the floor of his office, for God's sake; in the Senate Office Building. Sex and the democratic process, semen spilled in the sanctified halls of government. Just another fucking politician.

Now, ten months later, their affair was nearly as intense as it had been that first night. But both of them knew it would not last indefinitely. They were not in love, and each was aware of that fact; there was no feeling of commitment, no spiritual communion or understanding; they never spoke of the future. Passion was all, but passion dies and rekindles elsewhere. A few more months, maybe as many as six, and then there would be someone else for her and maybe someone else for him. End game. No recriminations. And that was the way it should be.

Tracy finished her drink and sat forward in the wicker chair. "I just can't seem to sit still," she said. "David . . . ?"

"Mmm?"

"Have you ever been bothered by trespassers out here?"

He frowned slightly. "Summer explorers and deer poachers once in a great while. Why?"

"I don't know. Maybe this stillness is getting to me, but I keep thinking about those missing guns."

"Come on, Ty. You explained that yourself: Jonas took them."

"You didn't seem very convinced of that."

"I'm convinced. No sign of prowlers in the house, was there?"

"No."

"Case closed. Another drink?"

"I don't think so. Why don't you show me some of the island? Those cliffs we saw coming in looked interesting. Maybe if I get to know the environment a little better, I'll feel more secure."

The suggestion appealed to Jackman; it had been such a long while since he had communed with the island himself. "Guaranteed," he said. "We've still got more than two hours of daylight left. That's plenty of time to go all the way to the cliffs, if you won't mind a two-mile hike round trip."

"My mother always told me I came from pioneer stock."

"Then we're on our way."

They got light jackets from their luggage, in deference to the evening cool, and then took the path up across the inland edge of Eider Neck and into the woods. The trees—mostly pine here, with a few spruce and balsam—grew thick and tall, and the light within the forest was dusky. The earth lay concealed beneath fallen needles decomposing into black humus. Green and gray moss-covered trunks and down logs and big gray outcroppings of rock, and clumps of lichen hung from spindly lower boughs. There was more sound here than there had been at the house: the light southeast wind murmuring among the foliage, the occasional chatter of birds, squirrels scurrying, the soft crunch of their footsteps. The air was heavy with pine resin and the odor of decaying wood. Tracy relaxed almost immediately; she was hardly the skittish type, and the shadowy woods seemed not to bother her. Before long, neither would the stillness or the city-bred fear of prowlers.

Nostalgia crowded his mind as they walked. He and Dale playing day-long games of hide-and-seek among these trees; the Old Man's nature and botany lessons; the excursions to the long flat top of the cliffs, to pick basketsful of the blueberries and strawberries that grew wild there; the low-tide explorations of the caves carved out of the cliff base by eons of crashing surf. God, how good it had been then, how simple, how innocent. What you believed in as a child was so much better than what you knew to be the truth as an adult—and wasn't what mattered then, at the base level, so much more important than what mattered now? Wasn't faith and love and beauty and simplicity what made up the soul of Man?

After they had gone a mile or so, the terrain began to slope steadily upward. The trees thinned and gave way to patches of open ground. Where the path skirted one of several fern-brakes on the island—a mini-jungle of brownish ferns, young pines, dead trees and branches like splintered gray bones—they paused to rest.

Tracy said, "This is a regular wilderness. I didn't expect anything like this."

"Do I take that as a favorable comment?"

"Absolutely."

"Wait until you see the cliffs," he said.

The path rose higher, through a long cathedral of trees, and then crested onto the flat. Acres of high green grass, dwarf pine, red-leaved blueberry bushes, multicolored wild-flowers—and beyond, the cliffs and the offshore islets nested by gulls and sandpipers, and the wind-crinkled sea stretching away to the horizon. To the west, the rim of the sun had dipped below one of the other large islands, but its rays were still strong enough to lay a firelike glow on the water and to bathe the flat in soft gold light.

"See what I mean?" Jackman said.

"It's beautiful, David."

"The most beautiful spot on the island, particularly at this time of day. I used to come here sometimes just to watch the sunsets."

He took her hand and led her across to the edge of the cliff, to where they could look down a hundred feet to rock walls and boulders made black by rockweed and algae and barnacles, white-edged waves hissing spray as they broke. They stood in silence, watching the movement of the ocean, and Jackman felt—not for the first time—a kind of mystical connection with it. It had always been for him a symbol of vast power and vast knowledge, considering what it was capable of and what it harbored in its depths; he imagined that it was a link between man and infinity, and that you could, if you watched it and listened to it long enough, comprehend some of the secrets of life and the universe, and thereby touch infinity itself. And maybe that was what every human

35

being was trying to do, in one way or another: live his life, play his games, and touch infinity once before he died.

He said this to Tracy, on impulse, and she did not laugh (Meg would have laughed). Instead she said, "Maybe it is. Maybe that's why men have been going to sea for millennia, and why they'll keep on doing it for as long as the world lasts."

"Yes, exactly," he said. "You know, I'm glad I brought you here. Not everyone would understand the island, or how I feel about it and about the sea."

She nodded but said nothing, staring down along the face of the cliff.

"There are caves below," he told her. "How do you feel about spelunking?"

"I love it—but not in caves."

Smiling, he said, "There's a way down that's not too dangerous. We could try it tomorrow or the next day."

"*You* can try it. I'll just watch, thanks."

"Coward."

"When it comes to scaling cliffs, right on."

They stood for a time in silence. The sun sank lower in the west, until more than half of it was hidden and the firelight paled on the water. "It'll be dark in an hour or so," Jackman said finally. "We'd better get on back."

They turned and started back across the flat. And something Jackman had not noticed before, because of the angle at which they had come out of the trees and because his attention had been focused on the sea, caught his eye. It was a pile of stones, curiously shaped—from this distance, not dissimilar to a barbecue—and it stood on a hump of ground in close to the pines. Jackman had never seen it before.

Tracy noticed it at almost the same time. She said, "Did you used to have cookouts up here?"

"No," he said, and went over in that direction.

When he neared the stone pile he saw a small shape lying in the hollowed-out center of it. And then recognized the shape and stopped abruptly. A red squirrel, laid out on its back, eyes like bits of black glass reflecting the dying sun.

Freshly disemboweled.

Tracy said, "My God," and Jackman felt her fingers dig into his arm.

A chill melted down between his shoulder blades. He took a step closer, and a second. Deeper into the hollow, at right angles to the dead and bloody squirrel, were a series of smooth yellowish-white spots. There was nothing else anywhere on or within the stones.

"David, what—"

"An eagle, maybe. There are eagle aeries on a couple of the islands in this area."

"An eagle wouldn't do something like that, would it? Eat the . . . guts of its prey and nothing else?"

"It might," he said. "And it might have been carrying the carcass back to its nest and dropped it here or left it here for some reason."

"Were these stones here the last time you came?"

"No, but Jonas could have built the pile since then."

"Why would he?"

"I don't know."

Tracy shivered slightly in the cooling wind. "I don't like this, David. It makes me twice as uneasy."

"You're not thinking of prowlers again—"

"Aren't you?"

Jackman said nothing. He continued to stare at the rocks, at the squirrel. The red-furred belly of the animal appeared to have been cut open, he thought then, not torn open by the sharp beak of an eagle. There was no other wound of any kind. Slaughtered alive, then.

After having been caught in some kind of snare?

And those yellowish-white spots—candle wax?

The chill on his back deepened. Up close like this, the arrangement of stones looked not like a barbecue at all.

It looked like a kind of altar.

DUSK WAS SETTLING when they hurried out of the woods and across the meadow toward the house, the warmly beckoning lights in the parlor windows. The western sky had an apricot tinge, and the wan face of the moon seemed balanced on the inland treetops; thick night shadows crowded the forestland, gave the evergreen boughs a charred look. To the northwest, at least two miles distant, another light on another island showed blurrily through the twilight.

When they reached the porch steps, Tracy hesitated—as if she were not certain the house was as empty as they had left it. Jackman went up ahead of her and opened the door and walked through into the parlor. Their bags still sat next to the couch, exactly as they had left them; the room itself still had the aspect of incompleteness, of perpetual waiting.

Behind him Tracy said, "No visitors while we were gone."

"Did you really think there might have been?"

"Oh don't sound so goddamned masculine-condescending," she said. Her voice was nervously sharp. She came forward, to within a pace of him, and stood searching his eyes. "We both know there could be someone else on this island. Not come and gone, but here right now."

"All right," he said, "it is possible. Jonas is careful about watching for trespassers, but someone could have slipped a boat in on the east shore and hidden it and themselves so that he didn't notice anything out of the ordinary when he made his final rounds. Or someone could have come ashore after he and his wife had already gone."

"And built that stone whatever-it-is and killed that squirrel and maybe got in here and took your father's gun collection."

"But damn it, I still think there's some innocuous explanation for all of that."

"Well, Jonas could have taken the guns, that's credible. But you don't honestly believe he's responsible for the squirrel and the pile of stones, do you?"

"It's also a possibility."

"Then why wouldn't he have left you a note explaining them?"

"It might have slipped his mind. He's an old man."

"If you had a telephone here—"

"But we don't have. Look, Ty, why would trespassers trap and then kill a squirrel? Why would they break into the house—and do it in such a way that there's no sign of forcible entry—and steal nothing but a collection of guns? It doesn't make any sense."

"Some people don't need reasons for doing things," Tracy said. "At least not rational reasons. Remember the Manson family?"

A corner of Jackman's mouth twitched. "Let's not let our imaginations run away with the facts."

"Things like that *can* happen, that's all I'm saying."

"Not on Jackman Island."

"David, we can't just ignore what we've found."

"We can if it's harmless."

"How do we find out either way?"

"Ty, let's look at this calmly. We've been here better than three hours now, and nobody's bothered us. We haven't seen anybody or signs of anybody except maybe for what we found on the cliffs. If there *were* trespassers, they're long gone."

"They could still be here, on the other side," Tracy said stubbornly. "Maybe they don't know *we're* here yet."

"If there were people on the island, they'd have to know about the house; know there are full-time residents. And if they meant harm, they'd be somewhere close by, waiting for the residents to come back—and they'd have put in an appearance by now."

"I don't want to stay here if there are trespassers, whether they mean harm or not."

39

"I still say we're completely alone and there's nothing to worry about," Jackman said. "There's just no evidence to the contrary."

"You're so damned confident," she said.

"I've been coming here most of my life, that's all, and there's never been anything to fear in all that time. This is *my* island; I'm not going to run away from it just because there may or may not have been trespassers in the past day or so." He paused. "If it'll make you feel any better, I'll take a look around outside. Check the storage barn and Jonas' cottage. If I don't find anything amiss, maybe it'll put your mind at ease."

"Suppose there *is* something amiss?"

"Will it make you feel better if I promise we'll take the boat and head straight back to Weymouth Village? Report strange goings-on out here to the authorities and let them handle it?"

"Yes."

"Then I promise. But it's not going to come to that."

"I'm going with you," Tracy said. "I'm not very good at sitting and waiting and wondering what's happening somewhere else."

He would have preferred to go out alone, but telling her that would only have indicated concern on his own part. And probably have raised hackles on the feminist in her as well. He said, "Tandem, then," and led the way out of the parlor and down the center hallway and onto the enclosed rear porch.

He opened a wall cabinet stocked with fuses and light bulbs and other household necessities. Took out two of four large-cell flashlights and handed one to Tracy. Then they went outside, into full darkness faintly silvered by the low-hanging moon.

There was nothing directly behind the house except a bare slope leading up to a line of trees a hundred yards away, and at the foot of the slope, a stone wall grown over with moss and ferns. Four feet high and extending parallel to the rear width of the house, twenty yards out on each side, the wall had been built as protection against heavy buildups of snow that sometimes led to slides in the winter. Jackman put his flash on and played the light along the length of the wall; then he went over and did the same along the opposite side. He swept the beam across the incline and up into the thickly shadowed woods.

Nothing anywhere except vegetation and emptiness.

They walked down to Jonas' cottage and circled it, Jackman checking doors and windows and finding each of them secure. He held the flash against the panes of three of the windows, one in back and two on the near side, bedroom and kitchen and parlor: clean, orderly, stocked with familiar anachronisms—Colonial cedar chest, horsehair sofa, Edward Howard Regulator clock, Chase trestle desk, each in its proper place.

"Everything's okay here," he said.

Tracy said, "Do you have a key?"

"No. There's never been a reason I should."

"I'm thinking about those missing guns."

"It's a pretty good assumption they're inside."

"But we won't *know* without looking, will we?"

"We're not going to break into Jonas' house, not without a better reason than that," Jackman said. "Even if the guns aren't inside, it doesn't prove anything. He might have taken them to the mainland. To a gunsmith for professional cleaning, something like that."

"I suppose so," she said, but her voice was dubious.

"The houses are undisturbed, that's the important thing," he said. "Now the storage barn."

They went back across the rear of the main house, flash beams cutting yellow patterns in the night. The wind hummed in the evergreen boughs, blew cold and already moist with sea mist over the open ground and against their faces. In one of the two apple trees that fronted the barn, a catbird imitated a robin's song and then followed with its own mewing call as if proudly identifying itself as a mimic. Summer insects made a faint pulsing wave of sound, like a distortional echo of what Maine natives called "the rote"—the sometimes muted, sometimes thunderous cadence of the sea breaking on rock.

There was no lock on the barn doors, and Jackman found one of the two halves slightly ajar when he and Tracy came up. Nothing unusual or sinister in that; if you didn't make certain the latch was firmly shut, the wind would tug it open. But he felt an involuntary tightening in his stomach as he widened the one half—and he swept his light over the shadowed interior without entering.

Cords of pine firewood against the back wall. Remains of the ancient carriage the Old Man had bought sometime in the mid-thirties with the impulsive and later abandoned idea of using it and an imported horse as island transportation. A stack of lobster pots and marker buoys and other gear which Jonas had stored here when he sold his fishing boat, the *Carrie B*, three years ago. Gardening and woodcutting and carpentering tools hanging within painted outline drawings above and beside the workbench along the left-hand wall. A bench saw and drill press. Five-gallon cans of extra gasoline. A pile of lumber in various sizes and lengths, including sheets of plywood. Roofing material. A farrago of discarded furniture and household odds and ends such as an old-fashioned top-coil icebox and a genuine wooden butter churn. And housed along the far-right wall, whirring softly, sending out faint vibrations, the heavy-duty generator which provided the island with its electricity.

Everything exactly as it should be; nothing missing, nothing added.

He said "Okay" to Tracy, and stepped back and shut the door, tested it to be sure it was completely latched. Then he looked up at the sky, at the soft moon and the bright cold stars; listened again to the commonplace night sounds; smelled the evergreens and the sea, the essence of the island itself.

Despite his assurances to Tracy, he had been edgy since their discovery of the disemboweled squirrel—and the edginess had increased as they searched the grounds. Hyperactive imagination, the power of suggestion. But now his stomach lost its tightness and the edginess began to disappear. He thought: Well of course it's okay. You expected it would be, didn't you? Nothing out here in the dark but the bête noire— old Mr. Bugbear. . . .

Ain't no bogeyman walkin round here in the dark, boy. Ain't no bogeyman, period. Nothin to fear at all cept old Mr. Bugbear, lives inside each of our heads. Mine, yours, he inside every person on this good earth.

Charlie Pepper. A night long ago, sometime in 1943 when Jackman was seven years old, yet vividly recalled even now. He had wandered away from the family home near Bangor, in search of frogs or salamanders or something else equally boyish, and had lost track of where he was along the river, and when nightfall had crept up on him he realized suddenly that he wasn't sure of how to get home again. There was an old mill on the river a mile or so from the estate, and some of the kids said it was haunted, and that the haunts would bite the heads off little kids who ran around alone in the dark. He sat down under a tree and imagined he saw haunts and bogeymen and other terrible creatures hiding in the shadows, and he cried and trembled with fear. And that was when Charlie Pepper had found him, wiped his eyes dry, and told him about old Mr. Bugbear.

Can't hurt nobody, old Mr. Bugbear, just talks and carries on. But if we listen long enough, he make us tremble and shake, make us see things ain't there, make us afraid and keep us afraid long as we let him do it, till maybe we end up hurtin ourselves. But when old Mr. Bugbear starts to talk, and we should stand up strong and say, Look here now, I know it's you and I ain't gonna listen—why, he got to shut up and leave us alone. So there ain't never any reason to listen to him, boy, you just remember that. Ain't never any reason to be afraid of what you don't know or what you don't understand or what you only think might be.

Quite a man, Charlie Pepper, in his own quiet way. A huge black who had, until his death in 1960, worked for the Old

Man for thirty-odd years as a chauffeur and general handyman. Who had spoken seldom and then mostly in a conventional Negro dialect, but who read W. E. B. DuBois and Langston Hughes and Richard Wright, among a number of other black and nonblack writers. Who looked a little like Stepin Fetchit and sometimes appeared to act a little like an Uncle Tom, but who fought all his life for equal rights through the offices of the NAACP, and maintained a great personal dignity which anyone who cared enough to acknowledge his humanity could recognize; the stereotypes existed only in the eyes and minds of bigots and fools. Who had had—Jackman hadn't quite grasped this until his midteens—an intense love-hate relationship with the Old Man, because each understood and grudgingly respected the other: master gamesman-by-design, master gamesman-by-necessity-for-survival. White king, black pawn—but on the gameboard they had been equals, and their thirty-year match had ended in a draw.

Jackman felt himself relaxing again. And as he relaxed, it occurred to him that in a perverse way he had been enjoying the melodramatics of the situation; had been stimulated by it, just as he had been stimulated by the island games he and Dale had played as children. He smiled wryly and said to Tracy, "Mr. and Mrs. North."

"What?"

"Fictional detective team. That's us—Pam and Jerry, out with our flashlights, searching for clues in the dark."

"David, don't for Christ's sake joke."

"Oh come on, Ty," he said. "We've been over the grounds and there hasn't been anything to find."

"And I'm supposed to be satisfied, right?"

"Meaning you're not."

"I don't know what I am except nervous."

Jackman took her arm and they moved back toward the rear of the house. When they got to the porch he said reluctantly, "Look, if it bothers you that much, we'll take the boat and put back into the mainland."

44

She did not say anything until they were inside the well-lit parlor. Then, turning to him: "I suppose you think I'm being a damned shrinking violet."

"You're anything but a shrinking violet."

"Normally. I'm a city person and I can cope with most of what a city throws at me; but I guess I'm out of my element here. That pioneer stock I told you about is so much crap."

"I won't think worse of you if you want to leave."

"But you'd be more than a little disappointed," she said. "It's pretty evident how you feel about this island."

"I won't deny that."

She studied him. "You wouldn't stay a minute if you thought there was really any danger, would you?"

"No, of course not."

Tracy turned abruptly and went over to the bar and began mixing herself an old-fashioned. "I hate weakness and I hate indecision," she said. Then, "Oh shit, David, don't pay any attention to me. We're not going back to the mainland until Monday afternoon. We're not going to spoil this week-end—*I'm* not going to spoil it."

"You're sure that's how you feel?"

"Reasonably sure. Okay?"

"Okay."

He joined her at the bar. He felt relieved at her decision, and relieved too at the sudden dissipation of tension that came with it. "Make me a drink, barman," he said. "Then I'll build us a fire on the hearth for the evening's pleasure."

"Bar*person*," she said.

"Oh? Was I being sexist again?"

"You were."

"Tell me, do you suppose I'd get more of the feminist vote if I changed my name to David Jackperson?"

"Nuts," Tracy said, and made a face at him. "Who's going to make dinner?"

"I will, tonight. How does roast squab, asparagus vinaigrette and Caesar salad sound?"

"Great."

45

"We'll have it when we get back to Washington. Tonight it's ravioli and stewed tomatoes and whatever else we happen to have in cans."

"Typical politician." She handed him a rum tonic. "Promises the moon, delivers a hunk of stale green cheese."

For a moment, that remark bothered Jackman; there was a hint of mockery in her tone—a trait he disliked, and which she exhibited often enough to irritate him. But then he shrugged it away and lifted his glass. He gave her a passable imitation of a Bogart leer, lowered his eyes to her breasts. "Here's looking at *yours*, kid," he said.

THEY SAT INDIAN fashion on the floor in front of the fireplace, backs against the leather couch, Tracy with her head on his shoulder. Pine logs blazing on the hearth made muted crackling, popping sounds, like sporadic bursts of distant gunfire; the only other sound in the parlor was the iterative ticking of the grandfather clock. All the lights were off, and the fireglow turned their faces and the room around them into a combination lightshow and shadowplay.

After Jackman had made sure that all the doors and windows on both floors were secure, at Tracy's behest, they had stuffed themselves with ravioli and Spam and tinned German pumpernickel, and had drunk a full bottle of Château de Viens '69 Bordeaux. He had hoped to recapture the light mood they had shared earlier in the day, because that was the way he wanted it between them here on the island. Uncluttered days and nights, untroubled thoughts. The proverbial weekend idyll. But while she seemed outwardly to have relaxed, he sensed that she was still a little uncomfortable; he

46

had caught her twice listening to sudden night sounds, cat-tense. Well, maybe she would snap out of it in the light of a new day—unless she was more like Meg than he might have thought, unless she was incapable after all of accepting the island for what it was. The prospect depressed him.

During the meal they had discussed filmmaking, the credibility of the auteur theory; he had lost none of his fascination for this career game over the years, and he seized every opportunity to pursue the subject. Now they were silent—Tracy seemed to want it that way; watching the fire and basking in its warmth.

He found himself thinking of other fires and again of other summers—and heard once more the ghostly echo of voices. The Old Man's voice in particular: resonant, stentorian, raised in anger, softened by humor, rich with wisdom, bloated with fool's rhetoric. Everything the Old Man had believed in and had been, politically and spiritually, had come from his own mouth in this room during one summer or another, spoken to his family or to guests of various persuasions. A partial, encapsulated oral biography of Thomas R. Jackman, retained by the walls of the house he had built, whispered in the night like the mutterings of an apparition in one of those legendary New England haunted houses. No chains here, no scrapings or rustlings or wailings or midnight walks; only glossy orations played and replayed to the tunes of "Over the Rainbow" and "Twilight Time":

—FDR said a while back, "The country needs, and unless I mistake its temper, the country demands bold, persistent experimentation. It is common sense to take a method and try it. If it fails, admit it frankly and try another. But above all, try something." Well, he's right, you know. No country and no individual ever gets anywhere without showing guts and backbone, without utilizing new tactics and fresh offensives. It's the by-God difference between winners and losers and always will be.

—That was a fine speech Marshall gave at the Harvard commencement, and this plan he and Truman have cooked up is a

47

damned good one despite the expense. But I tell you, Marshall made a mistake with that line about our policy not being directed against any country or doctrine. The major threat to Europe is Communism, and Marshall knows it and Acheson and Truman know it and everybody else in the country knows it. You can't keep skirting the issue; it's political suicide. Unless Truman and the rest of them lose their color blindness and start seeing Red where Red exists, Harry will be fortunate if he carries half a dozen states in the '48 election.

—Remember Youngman, owns that string of lumber mills in the northern part of the state, contributed heavily to my last campaign? He approached me just before I left the capital with a request for state funding on a ten-thousand-acre logging project. I see no reason why we shouldn't go along with him. If there's one resource we won't ever have to worry about exhausting, it's Maine timberland.

—You know that old story of Truman's: "Early on in my life I had the choice of becoming either a piano player in a whorehouse or a politician. And to tell the truth, there's not much difference between the two." Well, if I'd been faced with the same choice, I'd probably have made the same selection—unless of course it was a *first-class* whorehouse.

—I never took a dime under the table in all my years in public service, not a dime. But I don't mind telling you that I've taken a number of favors, and given a number more. There's nothing illegal or unethical in that. Hell, the entire political system would come to a grinding halt if everybody stopped scratching backs.

—Trouble with Kennedy is, he wants everybody to like him; he goes out of his way to get people to say "Well now, that JFK is a damned fine fellow." If he doesn't show a little brass and iron, and soon, people are going to realize he's too image-conscious to be a strong President. And that will be the end of him.

—Certainly I'm in favor of the U.S. intervention in Southeast Asia. The only game the Communists understand is force, I've said that for years. If we don't step in, Vietnam will fall and so will Laos and Cambodia and Thailand and Malaysia and eventually every other country in Asia. It's a tragic shame our boys have to lay their lives on the line because of this menace, but the cause of democratic freedom for all people is a just one. We should be proud and eager to do anything and everything we can toward that end.

—I'm delighted with my son's decision to enter politics; in fact, I don't mind taking some of the credit for it. All he needed was a little guidance from me, a little confidence in himself. He's the image of me when I was his age, you know: he sees things the same way, does things the same way. In the long run he'll turn out to be exactly the kind of congressman, exactly the kind of senator, that I was and have been to this day. . . .

"What are you thinking, David?"

Jackman smiled humorlessly, still watching the flames jump and dance around the dry pine logs. "About my father," he said. "Some of the things he said in this room, long ago."

"Things worth sharing?"

"No, not really." He shifted position; his right leg, prickling, had gone to sleep. "Political comments, mostly, and this is supposed to be an apolitical weekend."

"Mind and spirit free of Machiavellianism?"

"That's a pretty big word there."

"I know. And don't you just hate educated women? They're as bad as uppity niggers, right?"

"Oh shut up," Jackman said, and lifted her head and kissed her roughly.

He intended it to be a brief kiss, to tease her, but Tracy would not let him play that game. Her contained nervousness, seeking an outlet, made her aggressive; she laced both hands behind his head and held his mouth on hers, moving her tongue over his lips and then between them and hard against his tongue. Desire stirred in him and he held her more tightly, and she leaned into him and pushed him away from the couch and down flat on the rug, half on top of him, and took one of her hands away from his head and slid it down slowly between his legs. Began stroking him gently

49

with the palm. Her touch did not give him an erection—he no longer seemed to have instant erections, even with Tracy—but the desire deepened and his breathing quickened and his hands kneaded the curves of her buttocks.

He said against her mouth, "Why don't we go upstairs and continue this in bed?"

"What's wrong with right here?"

"It's not very comfortable."

"You didn't worry about that our first night in your office."

"Special circumstances."

"Mmm." She raised herself off him, kneeling, and started to unbutton her blouse. "Have you ever made love in front of a fire?"

Once, he thought, with Meg at her father's lodge in Massachusetts. But she was self-conscious about it, tightened up everywhere, and neither of us enjoyed it much.

"No," he said.

"Well I have. It's very nice."

"Is it?"

"You'll see," she said. She took the blouse off, and her bra off. Her breasts were medium-sized, the under curves deeply rounded, and the nipples and aureoles shone blackly in the firelight, like polished onyx. "Oh you'll see," she said. She reached down and unbuckled his belt and opened his trousers and stripped him from the waist down. Then she straddled him at the ankles. Her fingers touched his abdomen, cool and soft; moved downward in slow, diminishing circles until they centered on his groin, until he saw and felt himself begin to harden. Her eyes held his the entire time, her face a wicked mask of light and shadow.

And she said, "Shall I blow you, David?"

"Yes," he said.

"Now?"

"Yes."

"And you'll do me?"

50

"Yes."

"Slowly. Both of us—slowly."

"Yes. Yes. Yes."

They lay closer to the fire, spent, bodies heavy with the languor that comes with intense sexual completion. Jackman said, "Would you like to hear something not very funny?"

"What?"

"In all the years I've been married to Meg, we've never had oral sex of any kind. She considers it ugly and perverted, not to mention unsanitary."

"There's no accounting for taste," Tracy said, "you should pardon the vulgar pun. What turns one person's stomach, another gets off on. Perversion and pleasure are interchangeable, really."

"Meaning you condone sadism and the like?"

"Between consenting adults, as they say, why not? Isn't getting off, or the anticipation of getting off—not only physically but mentally—what really, basically keeps us all from reverting into savages, keeps us sane and in control of our lives? Life, liberty, and the pursuit of orgasm—that's the human way. When you stop to consider it, everything else is pretty empty and hopeless. We work and create for what? For posterity? For a better world tomorrow? Bullshit. What do we care about tomorrow's world? We'll be dead in another twenty or thirty or forty years, and it's those twenty or thirty or forty years that count because that's the only time we've got."

Jackman leaned up on one elbow. "Jesus," he said, "what turned on *that* metaphysical faucet?"

A crooked smile. "Sorry. I get carried away sometimes."

"Do you honestly believe what you just said?"

"More or less. Sometimes the human condition seems awfully damned pointless—or hasn't that particular little perception ever struck you?"

He lay back down. "It has," he said. Too many times, he

51

thought. "But there's still more to life, to human endeavor, than different kinds of orgasm."

"Such as?"

"Touching infinity, maybe."

"A form of getting off."

"Not if you believe in an afterlife."

"Which I don't. Do you?"

"I don't know. I used to."

"But now you're older and wiser—true?"

He shook his head. "I'm just not an existentialist, Ty. Living until you die isn't all there is. I wouldn't be what I am and where I am if I thought that."

"Well I hope you're right, David. Man ought to be *something* other that what he appears to be, have something more than self-gratification; but until somebody proves it to me, I'll just have to go on being a skeptic and a cynic. And believing that orgasm is the big enchilada, as a Hollywood friend says." She reached out to stroke his lower belly. "Speaking of which—do you suppose you can get that fat gentleman there to stand up again?"

Jackman had no further sexual desire; her egocentric philosophizing had robbed him of it. He was aware in that moment of just how little they had in common emotionally, of how shallow their relationship might really be at the core. Like his former relationship with Alicia, a totally self-centered woman—

But he did not want to think about Alicia.

He said, "No. Not tonight."

"Well how about if I hum 'The Star-Spangled Banner'? He'd have to stand for that, now wouldn't he?"

Jackman was not amused; the remark annoyed him instead. Wordlessly he got to his feet and padded naked to the bar and poured himself a brandy. He stood staring into it for a moment, then sipped at it without lowering the glass—what the Old Man had called "nibbling."

Tracy said, "Hey, did I say something?"

He turned. "No, it's all right. Want a nightcap?"

52

"Actually, I'd rather have a fuck."

That made him wince. The Look!-I'm-liberated language was just another of her less than endearing traits. He wasn't used to it from women, not so casually tossed out and not after having been married to Meg, with her proper Bostonian upbringing, for as long as he had. And maybe down at the core he was something of a prude himself, perhaps even the kind of male chauvinist Tracy teasingly accused him of being. The Old Man had been both of these things, of course, despite his extramarital affairs—

—and Jesus *Christ*, he thought, why do you have to keep bringing him into every memory or reflection lately? He's been dead for eight goddamn *years.*

". . . up to bed," Tracy was saying.

He shook himself. "I'm sorry, Ty, what did you say?"

"I said, since it appears I'm not going to be able to seduce you again tonight, we might as well go up to bed. It's gotten chilly in here all of a sudden, even with the fire."

"That's the fog," Jackman said automatically. "This is the time of night it starts drifting in from the sea. It seeps inside the house, no matter how tightly you seal it; you can't see it but you can feel it, the cold and dampness of it."

"Oh you're wonderful," Tracy said, and stood and began to hurriedly gather up their clothing. "You must tell lovely ghost stories. Now I'm not only cold and covered with goose-bumps, I'm being manhandled by invisible tendrils of fog."

He found a smile for that. "I'll protect you," he said.

They went upstairs and got into bed in the guest room. Tracy lay quietly beside him for a time, and he had the feeling she was looking at him in the darkness. Then he heard her sigh softly, and she began to rub against him for warmth. After a while, and after all, the rubbing and the softness of her body gave him an erection, and she said "Well, well" dryly and knowingly and rolled on top of him, and he entered her, and not long after completion he went to sleep holding her that way, still imprisoned inside her.

And as he slept he dreamed, adrift within himself in the

peculiar, almost cinematic way of all his dreams: both partici-
pant and narrator. . . .

*I have just graduated from college and I am visiting the Old
Man in Washington and I tell him I do not want to go into politics
as has always been tacitly supposed between us, that the success of I,
Camera, Eye at Cannes and on the art-theater circuit in New York
and San Francisco has convinced me to enter a career in filmmaking. He is silent for a long while and then he says "No," just that
one word, "No," and I realize with sudden agony just how much
influence he has, how many people owe him favors, and I know there
is no way I can win this game, I have no real choice except capitulation; and while he begins eloquently and persuasively to point out
why I must continue his work, I weep inside for what I am unable to
be and for what I will become*

*and it is my first term in Congress, my first full year in Congress,
and I am sitting at my appointed place on the House floor listening
to a roll-call vote on a bill to ban handguns from all but public and
private police agencies. Up and down voting, so I cannot abstain.
When the clerk calls "Jackman of Maine" I stand—but before I can
speak the members around me begin to laugh, and the clerk and the
Speaker join them, and within seconds everyone in the chamber,
members and guests alike, are on their feet and pointing at me and
the combined sound of their laughter is thunderous, reverberating
from wall to wall. I cannot understand why they should be laughing,
and I look around and then down at myself, and I am naked. I am
standing there naked and my penis is so shriveled that it appears to
be crouching, hidden within my scrotum, and it is at my genitals
that everyone is pointing, the source of their wild mirth. Then, before I can flee in shame, someone rushes onto the floor, I do not see
who it is, and shouts something, and the laughter stops instantly,
and he shouts it again, and this time I hear: he is shouting that the
President has been shot, the President has just been shot in Dallas*

*and I am on the first of my two visits to Vietnam, a Senate fact-
finding mission during which I have gone to My Lat and Chu Lai
and several other places, and now I am back in Saigon. There are
half a dozen of us—Senator Lawton from Iowa and three aides and*

54

a lieutenant from the Armed Forces Radio and Television Network—grouped outside a building in which we have just finished taping a television program: Lawton and I discussing the sentiments of the people at home, a brigadier general denying the widespread use of drugs among enlisted personnel and the rumors that innocent Vietnamese civilians are being slaughtered during searchand-destroy maneuvers. We stand sweating in the thick tropical heat, watching the ebb and flow of life around us, and then there is a sudden concussive sound and the sidewalk shudders under my feet and someone screams and there is a pall of smoke and someone else screams, and when I regain my senses I know that either a plastique bomb or a grenade has exploded. I see that none of us is hurt, none of us is hurt, but farther up the block a car is on fire and there are people lying on the street, women and children, and I run up there, shouting all around me, wailing, and I see a woman with no left arm, her left arm is propped against a fence ten feet away like something discarded, and near her is a child with blood all over him, so much blood I can't see his face, and I stagger and turn in mid-stride and run back again, away from all that, and I lean against the building wall and Lawton says Jesus that was close Jesus it almost got us, but all I can do is lean over at the waist and vomit, thinking It's all a game, it's all a game

and I am at a party in the home of Alan Pennix and I wish I was not there because I don't like Pennix, I don't like the politicians he controls or his reactionary policies; but it is the kind of Washington party which honors a visiting dignitary and which pretends to be apolitical, and Meg has insisted that we attend. I am in a corner, alone, one of those brief moments when you are between polite encounters with people who are trying too hard to play this game, or people like myself who wish they were engaged in another game altogether. I sip my second brandy, and Pennix comes up and with him is Alicia. This is Alicia, he says, and we talk and then Pennix drifts away and I am alone with her and I look at her closely, hair the color of the sun, good body, haunted eyes, oh haunted enthralling eyes, and I say I want to go to bed with you, Alicia, even though I know I am dreaming and in reality it did not happen quite like that, and she says Yes, David, and we go outside together and run through the night, we are naked and my genitals are shriveled but she does not laugh, she takes my penis in her hand and rubs it and says *You have a magic cock, David, when I rub it wondrous things happen,* and then she says *Now watch it grow, David, watch it grow, son,* and it grows and grows and now it is my turn to laugh and I enter her, we laugh together, we come together, and all at once she says *I want to be with you always, I want to marry you,* and I say No, we don't love each other, Alicia, and she throws a tantrum and screams that she is going to kill herself and I realize how unstable she really is, and then she is gone, she disappears, her landlady says on the telephone that she has moved out without leaving a forwarding address. I try to find her, I spend weeks trying to find her, but she has vanished and in the end I go home to Meg with my genitals shriveled again and Meg giggles when she sees them

and I am addressing the May Day demonstrators in 1971, but they will not listen, *We don't want words,* they say, *we want an end to that unholy war in Southeast Asia!* I want it too, I tell them, but my hands are tied, my cock is shriveled. *Then the country is dead!* they shout. No, I tell them, the country is alive; as long as we're free, we're alive. *Then we're dead for sure,* one of the demonstrators says, *because this is a goddamn police state, a fascist dictatorship,* and I say You're wrong, you're wrong—and the police and the FBI agents and the CIA spooks come, a sea of blue uniforms and tan trench-coats and tattered cloaks and gleaming daggers, and arrest all the demonstrators, they arrest 7,400 demonstrators, and every one of the 7,400 shouts at me *Stop them, don't you see what they're doing, they're trying to arrest the world!* But I only stand there, I cannot move, I can only say It will be all right, you'll see, everything will be all right

and I am back in Saigon, kneeling beside the boy with the blood all over him. I brush it away frantically with my palms, pints of it, gallons of it, and finally his face becomes visible beneath the wet red stickiness, I can see his face at last, and it is mine, oh God it is my face. . . .

Jackman woke up: sat up in bed, panting as though he had run a great distance, sweat streaming off him and slick beneath his arms; his mouth tasted cottony, abrasively dry. He blinked in the darkness, rubbed at his eyes, wiped his face with part of the sheet. Then, as his breathing became normal, he realized that he was alone in the bed. He glanced automatically toward the bathroom door, but it was open and the light was off inside. Tracy must have gone downstairs for something—a snack maybe, a glass of milk or juice.

The luminous hands on the nightstand clock read 11:45, which meant he had been asleep no more than an hour and a half. He listened to the old house creak and groan and remembered that as a child he had thought it was talking to him, but he could never quite understand what it was saying. Now he knew its voice was that of the Old Man: those glossy, ghostly orations from the past.

He leaned back against the headboard and closed his eyes, but he was not going to be able to get back to sleep right away. Dream remnants still clung to the corners of his mind, like freshly spun spiderwebs. He had had these dreams before, but never all in the same night, one after the other as though they were part of a distorted montage of his life: half-truths and incomplete historical events, filled out with bizarre symbolism so that you could not always separate reality from pure nightmare. Or real fears from those manufactured by the superego. The dream game, an intellectual puzzle that usually required a shrink as opponent or teammate, depending on *his* bent.

—What is it that's really bothering you, Mr. Jackman?

—I don't know that anything really is.

—Of course you do. Part of it is your father, and part of it is the state of the world generally and this country specifically, and part of it is an intermix of Meg and Alicia and Tracy.

—And part of it is me?

—Exactly. Part of it is you.

But he would not see a shrink, because he *could* not.

He found himself thinking, by extension, of Alicia; the dream had implanted her too firmly in his mind for easy rejection. He could see her clearly: small, fragile, colt-brown eyes, sun-colored hair, mouth turned into a perpetual half-pout. And he could hear her voice as it had sounded the last time he saw her—her demands that he marry her; her false vows to marry Alan Pennix if he didn't because she thought it would hurt him if he believed he would lose her to a political opponent; then, when that ploy failed, her threat to kill herself because she could not live without him.

But she had not loved him; she had loved only herself. She was flighty, self-centered, unpredictable, and in most ways an emotional cripple. She lived in a Washington world of parties and affairs and behind-the-scenes political intrigues—a bright soap opera world where all the feelings were intense and all the defeats unbearable tragedies. She sustained herself vampirically on the passions of others, but she was incapable of giving anything in return. Not unlike Meg. Not unlike too many people he knew.

Continuing the relationship with her had been impossible, and the night he had told her so was the night she had threatened to take her life. He had not given the threat serious consideration, and yet when she disappeared so suddenly a week later, he had developed the nagging guilt-oriented fear that she had, after all, committed herself to that childishly dramatic act. The fear had grown, would not give him peace, and he had expended a great deal of time and effort in trying to locate her. But she had no close friends and no family—her widowered father, an ex-ambassador to Nicaragua, had died in 1971—and the search had been futile. For all he was able to learn, she might have vanished off the face of the earth.

After two months he had been so emotionally drained and his nerves so frayed that he had become frightened of a breakdown. And so he had gone into a private hospital in Virginia for two weeks of rest. Quietly, so as not to alert his political opponents who would have found ways to use it against him, or those faithful constituents who equated such visits with serious mental health problems. He had not told

58

Meg (she would have been horrified), or anyone else. Instead he had carefully fabricated a fishing trip in the Canadian wilds, and the truth had not leaked out.

While he was in the hospital he had not been able to discuss Alicia, or the Old Man, or the dreams, or anything else of a personal nature with the resident doctors. He was only able to bring himself to plead overwork and constant pressures as the reasons for his presence there. The simple fact was, there had been no one in his life to whom he could talk, and he no longer had the capacity to bear his soul to *anyone*, least of all to a stranger. Despite John Donne's famous line, he was an island unto himself (one of the reasons, perhaps, why he had always felt a oneness with Jackman Island); he played the David Jackman Game within the boundaries of self.

Those two weeks had calmed him, eased his mind and conscience; for a long while after he came back to Washington—all through his difficult campaign for reelection, into this year—he had not been plagued by guilt and his sleep had been dream-free. In the past few months, however, despite almost daily doses of Librium and having given up smoking and coffee, he had begun to regress. And there was fear in him again. . . .

Jackman's mouth was very dry. He forced his mind away from these painful considerations and thought of joining Tracy in the kitchen for something to drink. Which was where she was, because now he could hear her rattling dishes down there. He got out of bed and put on his trousers and shoes. His shirt was not there: Tracy must have used it for a makeshift housecoat.

While he was dressing he looked out the window and along the rear of the house. The fog had come in thickly, a low furry ground fog that undulated and curled around trees and the barn and the long retaining wall. In places you could not see the earth at all. The moon, high above the evergreens, barely discernible from the window, painted the sky and

59

landscape a shiny silver and made the mist seem almost luminescent. The whole effect was eerie, unreal, but to Jackman comforting in its familiarity.

When he had his belt fastened he started to turn from the window, and something—movement—caught his eye and drew him back. It had come, or seemed to have come, from his left, between this house and Jonas' cottage. He stared out again, but nothing moved now except the floating carpet of fog. His breath misted the glass and he wiped it clear again with a palm, still did not see any further motion. A deer, maybe. Or his imagination again.

He went across the room, extended his arm toward the knob on the closed door.

Someone screamed.

Down in the kitchen someone screamed.

Tracy screamed down in the kitchen.

It brought him up short with his hand on the knob, froze him there for an instant because people did not scream in this house. Laughter, yes. Tears, yes. But no one had screamed here since it was built and no one should be screaming here now; this was the island, no one screamed on the island—

"David! David, *David!*"

He opened the door and began to run.

WHEN HE REACHED the bottom of the stairs, caught the newel post and swung around toward the archway, he saw Tracy come running into the parlor from the center corridor. He stretched out a hand as he passed through the arch, flipped the light switch on the wall; bright illumination flooded the room from the twin chandeliers, made him blink and then squint. They came together near the couch, and she put her palms flat against his chest as though she was not quite able to stand without aid. Her eyes were wide, her face darkly flushed; his shirt, the only thing she wore, was unbuttoned half-way down and her breasts heaved with the labor of her breathing.

"For God's sake," he said, "what is it, what happened?"

"There was someone . . . at the kitchen window."

"What! Are you sure?"

"I saw him, David, I was putting the orange juice away in the fridge and when I glanced over he was there. Looking in, with his face pressed to the glass."

"Did he try to get inside?"

"No. He was just standing there looking at me, smiling at me. His eyes were big as eggs, they didn't seem to have any pupils—"

Like Little Orphan Annie, he thought incongruously. He felt lightheaded; what she was telling him sounded as surreal as his dreams.

"—wild eyes, the kind you see on somebody who's heavy into dope. He was on something, David, I'd swear to it."

"All right, just take it easy."

"He stood there when I screamed," Tracy said, "and stood there when I shouted for you. Then he was gone. I looked out and saw him running toward the cottage, kind of bounding the way an animal runs."

"Animal?"

"I don't know, an animal or a person in one of those slow-motion TV commercials, you know what I mean."

Surrealism. "What did he look like?"

"Young, twenties somewhere. He wore a beard."

"You didn't see anyone else?"

"Isn't one enough? God, I knew there was somebody on the island—I *told* you. . . ."

He shook his head: a reflex movement. I was so sure there was nobody here, he thought. Then he thought: Old Mr.

Bugbear—and he said again, "All right, calm down. There's no point in making more out of this than necessary. We don't know who he is or what he wants."

"I don't *want* to know. I saw him, you didn't."

"We're in no immediate danger. He didn't try to come inside, you said that yourself."

"Not this time. But what's to stop a next time?"

"I'd better go out and see if I can find him."

"David. . . ."

"Got to be done," he said, and stepped around her and went out of the parlor, down the hallway and onto the rear porch. Foul-weather oilskins hung on pegs beside the door. He put one on, mostly just to cover his naked torso. Then, from the wall cabinet, he took down one of the flashlights they had used earlier.

Tracy had followed him; she said, "You'd better take some kind of weapon," in a shaky voice. "A knife or something."

"Why? He didn't have a weapon, did he?"

"Not that I could see—"

"Then there's no reason to assume he's armed."

"No? Are you forgetting those missing guns?"

A tic jumped along his jaw. "Lock the door when I go out," he said. "I'll come back in through the front with my key."

Jackman opened the back door and went out before she could say anything further, paused as she slammed it after him. The lock clicked. He felt oddly detached, angry at the violation of the island's sanctity, a little confused. He knew Tracy wanted to leave immediately, take the boat and head in to Weymouth Village, but he was not ready to give in to that, not just yet. The idea of running away was still distasteful—and from what would they be running? A young bearded man who may or may not be on dope; an apparition in the night, a Peeping Tom, a trespasser who had shown no indication of malice toward either of them. He had never been afraid of or antagonistic toward young people, as so many of his generation seemed to be these days; he had always managed a certain sympathetic rapport with the frustrations and

62

ideals, if not always the methods, of the subculture. And this was *his* island, damn it; his was the position of authority here.

But he could not exercise that authority unless he found the intruder; and he realized that he would not find him unless the man wanted to be found. The island was too large, the night too full of deep shadows and clever hiding places. All of which meant, then, that he might be left with no choice except to give in to Tracy's apprehension and take them back to the mainland. It would be foolish to do anything else. If he were alone here, perhaps—but not with Tracy as his responsibility.

He put the flash on and stepped away through the eddying ground fog: it came up nearly to his knees, so thick that he had the sensation at first of wading in gray liquid. The night's chill penetrated the oilskin, put goosebumps on his skin, numbed his bare ankles and insteps where they were exposed between trouser legs and shoe tops. The moonlight added a frosty violet tint to the sky, whitened the trees and the buildings, provided him with clear visibility.

He went around the northern corner of the house and halfway down toward Jonas' cottage. There, he stopped and looked across the front of the house, over to Eider Neck, along the rim of the bay, back to the beach where thin fog-crusted waves licked phosphorescently at the shale chunks and cobblestones. Stillness, save for the faint sibilance of the ocean. Everything frozen in stark relief, moon-drenched, carpeted in shiny mist.

Walking again, he swung the flash slowly from left to right. Threads of fog capered in the beam like will-o'-the-wisps. When he reached the front corner of the cottage, he stopped again and listened and heard nothing but the sea; even the wind was silent now. He walked around the edge of the porch at a measured pace, along its railed front—and came to another halt, abruptly this time. The hackles went up on the back of his neck; his groin knotted. He turned his head fully toward the cottage entrance.

There was something up there, sitting in front of the door.

63

And something smeared across the door and part of the wall beside it.

Jackman put the light up, held it still. His stomach jerked and bile pumped into the back of his throat. And he just stood staring with a kind of sick fascination.

What was sitting in front of the door was the blood-spattered head of a fawn, the eyes huge and terrified and reflecting the light like disks of polished milk-glass. The fawn had been a male: its severed genitals were visible where they had been stuffed into one side of its open mouth.

What was smeared on the door and wall was blood, the fawn's blood, and it formed both a crude cabalistic sign totally alien to him and the letters of a word. The word was:

LUCIFER!

Another five seconds went by while Jackman stared; then he made a sound of anguish and disgust and wrenched the light and his gaze away. Chills raced along his back and the bile taste was stronger. For the first time he felt real anxiety, the beginnings of genuine terror.

He turned and fled straight back to the house, onto the front porch. Fumbled his key into the lock, went inside, shut the door and leaned back against it. Icy sweat rolled down from his armpits and along his side. Don't panic, he thought. There's no cause for panic.

Footsteps overhead, hurrying along the upstairs hall to the head of the stairs. Tracy called warily, "David?"

"I'm here," he said. His voice was calmer than he had expected it would be.

"You didn't find him, did you?"

"No." He went up the stairs, arranging his face into a mask so that none of what he had seen and what he had felt would show through. When he got to the landing he saw that she was already dressed; her face was pale now.

She said, "I can't stay here any longer, David; I can't handle this kind of situation. I need people around me tonight, lots of them."

64

"You're right," he said. "You've been right all along. We'll take the boat."

"Now?"

"Soon as we gather up our things."

In the bedroom, while he shed the oilskins and put on his shirt and socks and jacket, she closed and fastened the catches on their bags. Then they went downstairs and out onto the porch, walked rapidly across the lawn and onto the path that skirted the beach—Tracy as though she were prepared to break into a run at any second, Jackman holding himself and his strides in careful check. No one pursued them. No one revealed himself.

He was sweating when they reached the boathouse door. Beside him, Tracy breathed heavily and stood looking back over her shoulder; the house and the cottage, draped in fog, had dull-white sheens, as if they had been dusted with talcum. And then he got the door open and they stepped inside.

Only to stop again, abruptly—staring.

Tracy said, "Oh my *God!*"

The outer doors were wide open: the boat was gone.

PART TWO

Saturday, May 23: — THE ISLAND

What wouldst thou, waylayer, from me?
Thou lightning-shrouded one! Unknown one!
Speak, what wilt thou. . . .

—NIETZSCHE, *Thus Spake Zarathustra*

THEY SAT TOGETHER in the dark kitchen, at the long antique-finished cobbler's bench which served as a table, backs to one wall so that they could watch the hallway arch and the window over the sink. When they had come back from the boathouse forty minutes ago, Jackman had put on the low-wattage hallway lights but no others; that illumination combined with the pale moonglow filtering past the window curtains to soften the edges of the night shadows. The refrigerator hummed steadily to itself and the sink tap dripped every few seconds. Otherwise there were no sounds: the house, too, seemed to be listening and waiting.

After a time the grandfather clock in the parlor struck one o'clock. The single note echoed through the darkness, left a ghostly aftersound that Jackman thought he could hear for at least half a minute. He shifted slightly in his chair, eyes avoiding the butcher knives and flashlights they had gathered on the table. The feeling of surrealism was back with him again, stronger now, wrapped in a thin layer of fear. He still had himself under control, but it was mostly external—a facade of calm, his political face, as if this were another of the

69

crises he met and handled with aplomb in Washington. Inwardly, he was trembling and unable as yet to cope with the situation.

He looked at Tracy beside him, sitting stiffly, eyes staring straight ahead, and knew that she blamed him for what was happening here: he had been so complacently sure that evil could not touch Jackman Island, that the danger signs could be explained away normally; if he had agreed to leave with her earlier, they would be safe in Weymouth Village now. Unless the boat had been stolen while they were up on the cliffs; but even if that were the case, she would still think it his fault for having brought her here in the first place.

That burden of culpability—warranted or not—had joined with the fear to build a wall between them. The real test of a relationship was a crisis: if there was anything at all solid between two people, they would grow more aware of each other, grow closer together; if there was not any foundation, then they would realize that fact and it would be over. Just like that—finished.

So it was finished for them, beyond any doubt. And he was not surprised. Subconsciously, perhaps, the arrangement had begun some time ago to dissolve for him. It would explain his annoyance at certain things she said, certain of her character traits; and it would explain why, facing her now, he had no feeling of intimacy, no feeling at all beyond concern for their mutual safety. He was looking at a familiar stranger —and it was like being alone.

And yet, ironically, the fear also bound them together: a stronger and more basic emotion than any of those which had united them during the months of their affair.

When she seemed to feel him watching her and turned her head, her eyes looked like wells of ink in the gloom. Her lips, thin and tight, glistened blackly where she had moistened them with her tongue. She said, "I can't take much more of this, David. My nerves are raw already."

"Get up and move around a little," he said.

"Damn you, we have to *do* something!"

70

"I know that."

"There's got to be some other way off this island—"

"No. I told you at the boathouse there wasn't."

"What about a rubber raft or a rowboat?"

"There's nothing. And even if there was, the currents are unpredictable this far out from the mainland; we'd probably be carried out to sea."

"So we couldn't swim to one of the other islands."

He shook his head. "That water is like ice all year round."

She fisted her hands on the table and was silent for a time. Then: "Why don't *they* do something, for God's sake? They stole the boat, they've trapped us here, why don't they show themselves and get it over with?"

"They're playing games with us," he said.

"What?"

"Games. Cat and mouse."

"Why? Who are they? What do they want?"

"I have no idea," he lied.

The refrigerator made a clicking noise and stopped humming to itself. Tracy's head snapped toward it, swiveled back to Jackman; she wet her lips again. "That thing up on the cliffs—it was some kind of sacrificial altar, wasn't it. That's the only explanation for the squirrel that makes any sense."

He had not told her about the fawn's head, or the blood on the door and wall of Jonas' cottage and what it spelled out. "Maybe," he said. "We can't be sure."

"David, let's dispense with the bullshit, okay? You think that thing is a sacrificial altar, don't you?"

"Yes."

"Then that bearded freak at the window could be a devil cultist, isn't that right? There could be a whole goddamn coven or whatever it is they call themselves on this island right now."

Lucifer! And a fawn's head with its genitals stuffed inside its mouth. And the disemboweled squirrel. And the altar. He did not say anything, listening to the sink tap drip and then drip again seven seconds later.

71

"Well?" she said.

"It's just kids," he said carefully. "High on drugs, playing thrill games."

"You think that would make them any less dangerous?"

"Killing animals is one thing; killing people is another."

"Yes? Well what about people like Manson and Starkweather?"

He was silent.

"And what about all those kids who were taught how to kill in Vietnam?" Tracy said. "Taught how to use drugs and how to hate and how to lose their perception of right and wrong. Some of them had to turn on to all that horror, the law of averages says that, and now they're right back here in this country. Maybe devil worship is their big orgasm. Maybe they get off on human as well as animal sacrifices. What the hell, David, all the big respectable owners of this democracy, all the war profiteers, got off for ten years on the dead bodies of tens of thousands of Americans and Vietnamese. This is a sick fucking world sometimes, or are you too busy fostering your own image, like most of your asshole political peers, to worry about what's really going on?"

. . . kneeling beside the boy in Saigon, brushing away the blood, searching for his face beneath the blood, and his face is mine. . . .

He stood abruptly and went over to the sink and ran water into his cupped hands. Splashed his face as if cleansing it. She was right in this, too—and she had not needed the fawn's head and the bloody message in order to interpret the kind of nightmare they might be facing here. His comments to her replayed in his mind and sounded fatuous and condescending now; their relationship was over, yes, but that was no reason to begin treating her as a mental inferior, as a hysterical stereotype who needed false reassurances.

Turning, he looked across at the table, saw her as a silhouette sitting motionless behind it. "Maybe I deserved that," he said.

72

"And maybe you didn't." She drew an audible breath, heavy and tense. "The point is, it could be any kind of sick weirdo out there—and what's to stop him or them from killing us? They've got guns, they took your father's guns."

He came back to stand in front of the table. "We still don't *know* who and what they are, but there's no use lying anymore to myself or to you: we've got to assume they mean us harm. Which means the only way to survive is to play this game better than they play it, outthink them, outmaneuver them."

"Then we've got to decide what we're going to do right now."

Jackman said, "All right, we—"

And the door chimes went off.

Behind the table Tracy made a startled noise and her body jerked and she came up onto her feet as though in reaction to an electric shock. Jackman half spun and stared into lighted hallway. The fear crawled down through him and seemed to center in his genitals. Pulse thudded in his ears; there was a metallic taste in his mouth.

Tracy said, "God, David. . . ."

The chimes rang again, a sweet clear echoing melody—but as chilling in that moment as a music box playing in a sealed crypt.

He swept a flashlight and a butcher knife off the table. What sort of tactic was this? A subtle form of torture, like a drop of water on an exposed nerve? Or a diversion to take them to the front door so that access could be gained through the rear? Most likely the former, in which case whoever had pushed the door button would be gone by now, hidden again, watching. Countermove to the rear porch, then, just to be sure.

He stepped over beside Tracy, caught her arm with his free hand. "Stay with me," he said sotto voce.

When she nodded he led her out onto the enclosed porch and then motioned her to the wall on the unwindowed side

73

of the door. He took a place next to the window. Outside it was quiet, not a murmur of sound. From inside, the same: the chimes had not gone off again. He leaned his head toward the frame of glass—

In that same instant it exploded inward, spraying gleaming black fragments; something long and slender hurtled past Jackman's head.

He lunged backward, releasing both the knife and the flashlight and bringing his hands up, turning his head downward, closing his eyes—all of it instinctive. But there were needle-pricks of pain on his left cheekbone, under the right eye, above the right corner of his mouth. Dimly he heard Tracy stifle a cry, the shards falling like crystalline raindrops, the thud of whatever had smashed the window as it struck the inner wall and then dropped clattering to the floor.

He blinked his eyes open, and they were undamaged, he could see all right. The cuts began to sting, and when he touched his cheeks he felt the tear-stream wetness of blood, the gritty sharpness of tiny glass particles. He took the handkerchief out of his back pocket and dabbed and brushed gingerly at his face. His hands were trembling.

Tracy was talking to him, he realized, asking in an urgent whisper if he were badly cut. "No," he said, "I'm okay," and pivoted and looked through the frame of the window, past jagged edges of glass like unevenly serrated teeth in an open mouth. Breaths of cold air burned against the cuts, chilled the sweat on his forehead. In the silvery moonlight outside, the mist crept sinuously along the ground, concealing most of the stone fence, enwrapping the lower boles of the two apple trees as though in furry gray moss. For all he could see, it seemed now to have the night to itself.

Jackman picked up the knife and the flashlight, gave the latter to Tracy and put the weapon through his belt on the right side. Then he thought of the object which had been hurled through the window, and went over to the inner wall and knelt. Groped along the floor until his fingers touched it—but as soon as they did, he pulled the hand back. "Christ," he said softly.

Tracy said "What is it?" and dropped down beside him and clicked on the light.

It was not as bad as he had expected from the feel of it, but it was bad enough: a jagged piece of bone, probably from the slaughtered fawn, with bits of gristled meat clinging to it. There was something else clinging to it as well—a crumpled sheet of ruled paper, fastened on with a rubber band.

"They killed another animal," Tracy said sickly.

He nodded. Don't look at the paper, he thought. You don't want to know what's on it; Tracy doesn't want to know.

She looked at him as though reading his thoughts. He held her gaze for several seconds and then, because they both knew looking at the paper was unavoidable and inevitable, he swallowed bile and lifted the bone between thumb and forefinger. Took the sheet off of it, spread the paper open on the floor as Tracy lowered the flash.

The same cabalistic symbol, and letters fingerpainted in crimson:

YOUR BLOOD NEXT FOR THE CUP OF LUCIFER.

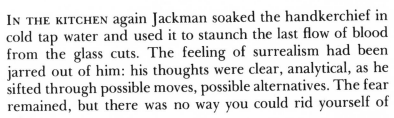

IN THE KITCHEN again Jackman soaked the handkerchief in cold tap water and used it to staunch the last flow of blood from the glass cuts. The feeling of surrealism had been jarred out of him: his thoughts were clear, analytical, as he sifted through possible moves, possible alternatives. The fear remained, but there was no way you could rid yourself of fear until you eliminated or deactivated its source; the problem was keeping it at a manageable level.

And the secret to that lay in continuing to think of all this as a game. A game not at all capricious, not at all created for the thrill of itself alone. A game not unlike those once held in the Coliseum in Rome for the amusement of the decadent masses, in which survival—thumbs up!—was the only purpose; in which the weaker would be destroyed—thumbs down! Every bit this kind of senseless and repulsive game, yes, but a *game* nonetheless. And the Old Man had taught him all there was to know about game-playing. . . .

When he came away from the sink Tracy said, "How much longer do you think we have?"

"No way to tell. They might keep on toying with us all night, or they might have already tired of it. Ty, the only option we've got that makes any sense is to get out of here, away into the woods. Now."

She stared at him in the pale stream of moonlight from the window. "You want us to go out there where they are?"

"It's twice as dangerous if we stay here."

"I don't understand that."

"We're vulnerable here."

"We'd be vulnerable out there."

"Not in the same way. Outside, at least we'd have places to hide, room to maneuver: we can make offensive moves as well as defensive ones. In here we're trapped, they know exactly where we are."

"Yes, but—"

From without, at the front of the house, there were sudden clanking sounds, dull and metallic and not quite identifiable.

Tracy said, "What was that?"

He shook his head, turned past her to look cautiously through the window. Moonlight and shadow. But he heard the sounds again, more distantly this time. Front lawn? Somewhere out there.

They were not repeated a third time.

76

At length Jackman said, "More scare tactics, maybe. Another turn of the screw. And this is only the beginning." He took her shoulders tightly in both hands, felt the ropelike tension in her muscles and tendons. "Ty, believe me—we've got to get out of here."

"I don't know. . . ."

He said, "There *is* a way off the island, if we can find it."

"What way?"

"*Their* boat. Christ knows what they did with the cruiser—set it adrift with the bilge plugs open, maybe—but whatever they used to come to the island has to be around the bay here, or at the cove on the east shore."

Tracy's throat worked heavily. "But *how* can we get out, David? They're right outside, they could shoot us down or run us down before we're able to get away. . . ."

"We'll create a diversion."

"What kind of diversion?"

"Give me a minute; I'll think of something."

"Then which way do we leave? Back or front?"

"Neither."

She said, "One of the windows?"

"No. There are outside storm doors on the south side of the house. We'll go down to the basement through the pantry, then up through those doors and into the trees beyond the barn."

"Then?"

"Cross-island to the cove," Jackman said. "It's the most probable spot for them to have landed; coming in, they couldn't have known the buildings here were deserted. And that way we make sure we're completely clear of them."

"But if that's where their boat is, they might realize we'd go there."

"Doesn't matter. I know this island; I can find my way over every inch of it, dark or light. No way they can get to the cove before we do—there's a shortcut. If we can keep them off our backtrail, we should have at least twenty minutes."

Tracy was silent for a moment, but he sensed that she was

with him now; the rising inflection in her voice was that of hope. She confirmed it finally by saying, "All right, David. Do we leave right away?"

"As soon as possible."

"What do we take with us?"

He considered that briefly. "One flashlight each. One knife each. I've got a pair of binoculars in my room upstairs that are made for night use as well as day. And we should have more clothing on than these light jackets and sweaters."

"We could wear those oilskins on the porch."

"Good. They'll make us more difficult to see even in the moonlight."

"How about food?"

"Some, maybe. Just in case. But nothing heavy or bulky. Only things that will fit in our pockets and not hamper movement."

"I'll take care of that."

He nodded, and without either of them saying anything else he went into the hallway and across the parlor. As he climbed the stairs to the upper floor, Jackman thought that they were interacting well enough now, functioning with the necessary teamwork to carry out the plan he had made. He was glad it was Tracy and not Meg, because Meg would have been totally helpless, she would have gone to pieces long ago.

And how about me? he thought then. Are *my* nerves going to hold up? Not bad now, because he was keeping his mind focused on the opening gambits of this Most Dangerous Game—but what if those gambits failed and the game became more intricate, dragged on and on?

One thing you've got to remember, son: make your moves one at a time, and be careful of looking too far ahead. More games are lost by overcalculation, worrying too much about what's coming up later on, and not paying enough attention to the next move on the board.

He blanked his mind, entered his old room and felt his way across to the tier of shelving on the opposite wall. And in the same moment he found the binoculars, he also found the diversion they would need to get out of the house: his old reel-to-reel tape recorder.

He stood for a dozen seconds, thinking it through. Then he uncased the glasses and looped the carry strap over his head, bent in front of the recorder and removed its top speaker cover. Enough moonshine penetrated the drawn curtains to show him that there was a tape on the two plastic reels, that the microphone was intact in its little compartment. The machine had not been used in a long time, years, and as he drew out the electrical cord and knelt to plug into the wall socket, he prayed that it was still operative.

When he straightened again and touched the ON switch, the time meter light glowed and the recorder made a soft humming sound.

Jackman released the breath he had been holding and rewound the tape, pressed the button for RECORD. The tape began to run, erasing whatever had been on it, but he did not speak into the microphone. He looked at the radium dial of his watch and timed a full five revolutions of the second hand. Then, finally, he said in his normal voice, "This is David Jackman, the owner of this island. I don't know who you are or what you want, but unless you get off my property right now I warn you there'll be serious charges pressed against you. Technically all you've done so far is to commit acts of vandalism and malicious mischief, but that note you wrote us could be considered a direct threat if I choose to interpret it that way. I expect friends on the island in the morning, several of them, and if you're still here by then you'll leave me no alternative except to have you hunted down and arrested. . . ."

He went on in the same vein for another two and a half minutes. Then he unplugged the microphone, rewound the tape again, shut off the recorder, packed it together, and stepped over to the window on the south wall. Below and toward the rear, he could see the dark shape of the storm doors. The moon-drenched ground between the house and the trees beyond the barn was deserted. He came back to the recorder, caught it up, and carried it out of the room.

In the foyer downstairs he put the machine on the antique table, then dragged the table to the right of the door and two feet behind it. Just as he finished, Tracy came hurrying in from the parlor, wearing one of the oils and holding a second draped over her arm. The deep pockets of the slickers bulged, not too fully, with foodstuff and the knives and flashlights.

She said, "What took you so long? I've been ready to jump out of my skin, waiting down here alone."

"Did you see or hear anything outside?"

"Those clanking sounds again. That's all."

Jackman opened the recorder, stood its speaker cover to one side. He said, "This is part of that diversion we're going to need."

She frowned. "Did you record something while you were upstairs?"

"A three-minute speech with a five-minute silence ahead of it," he said. "Those are the five minutes we'll need to get down to the basement and make ready."

"I hope that thing has good loud volume."

"It does."

He found that he had to move the table back another foot in order for the plug to reach the nearest outlet. He did not turn on the machine, just left it where it sat. To Tracy he said, "What I need now is some heavy twine, at least a hundred and fifty feet of it."

"What for?"

"I'll show you when we find the twine."

They went down to the kitchen again, Jackman putting on the second oilskin, and then rummaged through the cupboards and the drawers in the drainboard cabinets. He began to think they were taking too much time, that they should have been out of here by now—but that was the fear working inside him. He had to keep reminding himself not to play recklessly, not to let panic govern any of his actions.

80

Tracy found the twine, a large ball of it, in a utility drawer. He took it from her and motioned her to follow, and when they came into the foyer once more he skirted the table, unwound an end of the string, and tied it securely around the front doorknob. Unlocked the door, and turned the knob until the latch clicked. Eased the door inward fractionally and then backed off, paying out twine.

And the clanking sounds came again, very loud, very close off to the side of the veranda.

Jackman stiffened, saw Tracy raise a fist to her mouth as though to lock in a cry. Clank. Clank. Silence. Clank—

All at once, he identified the sounds, knew their source. He said "Jesus Christ," and felt a prickly cold settle across the back of his neck.

"David?"

"Gasoline cans," he said.

"What?"

"From the barn, Jonas keeps an extra ration of gasoline in there." He hesitated; then: "Maybe they've got it in their heads to set fire to the house."

Sharp intake of breath. "No," but it was a plea instead of a negative.

Clank.

Clank.

Fear and urgency prodded Jackman into motion. He moved closer to Tracy, gave her the ball of string. "Go back into the pantry and unwind this along the way. Hurry. I'll join you in a minute."

He watched her back away through the parlor, unraveling the twine. When she disappeared into the center corridor, he entered the parlor himself and looked out through the nearest of the south windows. Stillness. He came back into the foyer, considered opening the front door, decided it was too much of a risk, and listened.

Silence.

He switched on the tape recorder, pushed the PLAY button, and turned the volume up as far as it would go. The machine

81

hummed noisily; its lights glowed like tiny yellow eyes in the darkness. He pivoted away from it and moved silently back along the slack path of the twine, making sure there was nothing on which it could hang up once he pulled it taut.

When he came into the pantry, Tracy had already opened the basement door; she stood holding what was left of the string ball. He took it from her and put it on the floor just beyond the sill of the basement door.

Their was a sudden frenzied knocking on the back door—sounds that echoed madly in the stillness.

Tracy's fingers dug into his arm and he felt the bite of her nails. He did not say anything, did not hesitate; he pushed her through the door and followed after her and pulled it to behind him without latching it. Took the flashlight out of his slicker, clicked it on, aimed it down the stairs as they descended.

The basement was damp and cold and had the faint mold-like odor of any underground place long shut-up, long unvisited. The walls and floor were of concrete. Part of the facing wall was covered with hand-built wooden niches, pegged instead of nailed together, for the storage of the fine wines the Old Man had been fond of serving to his summer guests; only a few bottles filled them now. There were also two old casks on a wooden platform—so old that they had been wine-stained to a uniform black color—which a vintner had supplied in payment for some small favor. On another wall were shelves constructed to hold canned goods; all they held now was dust. Cobwebs hung like moss from the low wooden ceiling, spanned some of the supporting timbers in lacy gray patterns.

Jackman pointed the flash across to the far end, where the basement had been widened into a kind of annex that extended beyond the south wall of the house. Another set of wooden steps led up from there to the outer storm doors.

They went over to the annex, and he climbed the steps to the doors: two wooden halves that opened outward from the middle. Now that they were no longer used, heavy iron bars fitted through iron brackets held them locked against the gale-force winds that sometimes buffeted the island during the winter months. Jackman removed the bars, carefully, and carried them down and laid them on the annex floor.

Looking again at his watch, he said, "Seventy seconds. I'll do the twine."

"Should I go up the steps?"

"Yes. But don't touch the doors yet."

He ran back to the pantry stairs and went up and pushed the door open far enough to pick up the twine. Forty seconds. Carefully, he began to take up the slack, reeling it in like a fishline. Twenty seconds. He could feel himself sweating, beads of it breaking and running down off his forehead, stinging against the glass cuts on his cheeks; he half-expected to smell smoke, hear the crackle of flames, at any second.

Fifteen seconds. Ten. And the twine tightened, became taut: the front door was open. Jackman looped the twine around the knob of the basement door, to keep it stretched, and took the steps going down again three at a time.

"This is David Jackman, the owner of this island. I don't know who you are or what you want. . . ."

When he came up the annex steps beside Tracy, he said against her ear, "We'll give it a full minute, maybe a minute and a half. It'll take us less than ninety seconds to get from here into the trees."

"You'd better go out first when the time comes," she said. "You know exactly where to go."

"All right."

". . . you're still here by then you'll leave me no alternative but to have you hunted down and arrested. This game you've been playing is senseless and childish, you must realize that. We're not afraid of you. . . ."

"One minute," Jackman said. "Thirty seconds to go."

He moved around her, one step higher, and put the palms of both hands against the door halves. Stared at the sweep hand on his watch.

". . . what you expect to gain by all this? Kicks, thrills—is that

it? Does hiding in the dark like animals, terrifying people, give you some sort of warped pleasure. . . ."

One minute and thirty seconds.

"Now!"

He shoved the doors apart, pushed them back against their hinge stops so that they would stay open. Raised his body up and out between the halves and swung his gaze from left to right. Moonlit grass, the dark distant sweep of trees, the inner hump of Eider Neck, a long wedge of the front lawn: empty, all of it empty, but light that did not come from flash beams flickering around the corner, out front, out of his vision—and he levered himself off the top step and came out running.

He heard Tracy scramble out behind him, heard his own recorded voice eerily hammering away at the night from the front entrance; he wanted to turn his head, to look for pursuit, but he knew that would slow him and so he kept his eyes on the trees, head ducked down, shoulders hunched, you would never hear the shot that killed you, and then Tracy was beside him, running with him, reaching for and clasping his hand, and he increased the length of his strides, or thought he did, but the trees did not seem to come any closer. Blood pulsed in his ears and his breath sprayed between clamped teeth, he felt as though they were running like squirrels in a cage wheel, disemboweled squirrels, decapitated fawn, *". . . warning you, I'll see you prosecuted to the fullest extent of the law if you do not . . .," stumbling, sweating, and* finally, finally the woods loomed near, almost there, no shot, no sounds behind them—we're going to make it—and the elongated shadows cast by the first of the evergreens reached out and they rushed into them, blended with them, panting.

". . . only going to say this one last time. I won't toler—"

Jackman heard his voice cut off in mid-word, but the tape would not have run out yet and that meant one of them had turned off the recorder. He had to look back then, like Lot's wife: back and down across the expanse of open ground.

No one there, no one had seen them.

But from this angle he could make out the source of the flickers of light at the front of the house: fire, all right, but not the house—a cross, they had constructed a wooden cross on the lawn and then set it ablaze. It stood there burning within swirls of fog that looked, in the high shimmering glow of the flames, like mists of fresh blood. . . .

JACKMAN LED THE WAY deeper into the woods, skirting a fernbrake and then a small clearing dotted with deadfalls and seedling spruce. A third of the way around the clearing he sensed rather than saw the place where the path began, and picked it up almost immediately.

When the trail began to run in a narrow zigzag through forestland so dense that only patches of the moonlit sky were visible through the canopy of boughs overhead, he stopped abruptly and leaned against one of the pine boles. He drew Tracy in against him, holding tightly to her hand. "We can take time to catch a second wind," he said. "We've got a good jump on them."

She nodded and rubbed at the sheen of sweat and mist on her face. Seconds passed. Then: "How far to the cove?"

"Another third of a mile."

"Can we risk using one of the flashlights now?"

"We'll have to for maximum speed."

"David. . . ."

He looked down into her face.

Hesitation. Finally she said, "Nothing, there's nothing to say," and he knew she had seen and was thinking about the burning cross. And she was right: there was nothing to say.

They had rested long enough, he thought. He put on his

flash, angled the beam downward, and they took to the path again, walking rapidly instead of running now because of the jutting lower branches that were a constant danger to the eyes. The upper boughs swayed gently, almost rhythmically, as if to the beat of inaudible music. Fingerlike wisps of fog caressed their legs and lower bodies with damp intimacy.

In the distance Jackman could hear the hissing sound of the rote; the tide was at flood and the ocean restless despite the mild weather, the lack of any but a soft breeze. The open sea beyond the southern cliffs would be treacherous, impossible to navigate, which meant that they would have to take the boat around to the north and across to Little Shad Island and then back in to the mainland; you had to be careful off that side of the island or you would rip the belly out of your craft on one of the ledges—

If they had landed at the cove in the first place; been cautious and escaped the ledges and brought their boat in there instead of at the bay.

If there was a boat at the cove, and *if* it was one that did not require a key to start the engine, and *if* there had not been a guard posted. . . .

The evergreens thinned after they had gone a quarter mile, and the path led through a field of brown grass riddled with a network of narrow passages built by meadow voles, then up across a ridge of flattish rock and gnarled old birch, and finally down into more pines and spruce. From the east the sound of the rote was much louder now, and the pungent smell of seawater became greater than that of the forest. Jackman remembered that the path hooked around and came out of the woods on the western rim of the cove's wide, rocky beach. But you could leave the trail where it started to loop and continue straight ahead and exit at the trees on the northern lip of the beach, where there was a short multi-ribbed shelf of granite rock. Beyond the shelf was a natural stone dock, maybe sixty yards from the trees; anyone coming into the cove would see that dock and would not look any further for a place to moor his boat—there *wasn't* any other place nearly as safe or as accessible.

He shut off the flash as they came on a rise in the terrain—on the far side the land sloped sharply downward and then flattened out to the waterline—and said to Tracy, "We can't chance using the light the rest of the way. Once we top this rise, anyone at the cove might be able to see it through the trees."

"I thought you said they couldn't get there before us."

"They can't. But there's the possibility of a sentry."

Pause. "What do we do if there is one?"

"I'm not sure," he said.

"Overpower him?"

"Maybe. Something like that."

"Kill him if necessary? Could you do that, David?"

"If it means saving *our* lives, yes," Jackman said, and did not know if that was the truth or false bravado. How does a man know if he is capable of killing another man until he is put to the test? How does a man know *anything* about himself until something happens to force knowledge on him? Intellectually and spiritually you might consider yourself courageous, capable of dealing with any crisis; but physically or instinctually you might turn out to be a coward. Or vice versa. Dei judicium.

What am I? he thought.

"There won't be a sentry," he said, and shivered inside his slicker. He had not noticed it coming cross-island, but the night had grown very cold: the breath of wind against his face and hands had lost its late-spring softness and become instead hard and chill, as sometimes happened in the black, empty hours between midnight and dawn.

"I hope not," she said, "Jesus," and he looked at her but could not see her face beneath the hood of her oilskin.

Neither of us knows what I am, he thought, and maybe neither of us wants to find out.

They climbed to the high ground, picking their way cau-

87

tiously in the darkness, guided only by dapples and thin shafts of moonlight and Jackman's recollection of the path's course. The sound of their steps was cushioned by the damp humus underfoot, but now and then one of them would accidentally snap off a dry twig with some part of their body and the crack of it would echo through the silent woods. It would not carry far, though, and even if it did there were enough night sounds—falling cones, the scurrying of rodents and deer—so that it would seem natural and normal to anyone listening.

When they got to the place where the trail hooked toward the rear of the stone beach, Jackman took Tracy's hand and pulled her straight ahead through a tangle of ferns and bayberry shrubs. She followed without question or hesitation. After fifty yards he heard the slap-hiss of waves breaking over the rock shelf, and after another twenty he could see, through the trees ahead, torn patterns of fog drifting low across the shoreline.

Near the last verge of pine, he had a clear view straight out to sea. He could not make out the cove yet, any of the beach or the stone dock, because of the density of vegetation on their right. Out past the breakwater the mist was thicker, a long fluffy blanket that obscured part of the horizon. Above it, stars burned coldly, and the moon stared down like a whitish cyclopean eye; below it, a silver-tipped tier of combers rolled shoreward. The shelf and its hirsute coating of black algae glistened wetly with spray and tide pools.

Jackman stopped and said against Tracy's ear, "The footing gets a little precarious ahead, where you've got to go to see the cove. Maybe you'd better wait here."

"All right," reluctantly. "But not long."

"Not long," he said, and left her and went ahead until the earth beneath his feet gave way to slippery rock. Then he angled to his right and ducked past a cluster of wild cranberry bushes, came out at the inner edge of the shelf. The smooth rock was ten feet high here, too high to see over, and he moved around it vigilantly toward the beach. His foot slipped once on the slick surface and he went down hard to one knee, almost lost the flashlight but recovered in time and knelt there for a moment biting his lip against the pain in his kneecap. Chill spray from a breaking wave spattered the left side of his face, and its salt taste reminded him, oddly, of tears.

He pushed himself erect again and moved out to the beginning of the cobblestone beach, keeping his body humped over and pressed in close to the shelf. From there, then, he could look down across the beach to where the combers ran in, to where the natural dock jutted wet and mist-streaked from the inner wall of the shelf.

There was nothing there: no boat, no guard, nothing.

He swallowed thickly and scanned the beach and the rest of the cove. Emptiness. Lowering himself onto one knee, not the one he had fallen on, he raised the binoculars off his chest and adjusted the focus and swept the area again, slowly. But there was no place to hide a boat, no place to moor one within the cove or on either side of it out past the breakwater.

Jackman stood and turned back the way he had come, into the woods, to where he had left Tracy. She had hidden herself behind a tree, and when she saw him she came out and searched his face.

"It's not there, is it."

"No," he said.

"Then it's at the bay somewhere."

"Yeah. Eider Neck, maybe."

"So we've got to go back where *they* are."

"They won't find us, Ty."

"Suppose we can't find the boat?"

"We'll find it," he said.

Silence. And then she said, "I knew all along it wasn't going to be here," in a voice that was flat, controlled, but with an unmistakable undercurrent of despair. "I knew it wasn't going to be anywhere near that easy for us."

He said nothing. But he thought: Yes—so did I.

And for the first time, the very first time, he understood that they might lose this game: he stood face to face with his own mortality.

THE OPEN MEADOWLAND south of Eider Neck seemed to shimmer liquidly in the night wind, mist-fringed and shining as though frosted under the lunar glow from above. Seaward, a marshy area seventy or eighty yards wide at its deepest inland point stretched between the outer edge of the Neck to the wall of trees in which Jackman and Tracy now stood—a distance of some two hundred yards along the slightly convex shoreline. Except for part of the barn and the tip of the house roof, the island buildings were hidden behind the humpbacked peninsula. The sky in that direction was untinged by artificial light of any kind.

Jackman swept the area with the binoculars, did not see anything out of the ordinary. "We'll go straight across the meadow," he whispered, "and onto the Neck. Before we start looking for their boat, we've got to get an idea of how things look around the house."

"All right."

He took her hand and they moved rapidly out of the trees, slicker bottoms flapping against their legs like rubber wings. When they got to the foot of the Eider Neck slope, Jackman slowed and dropped onto his hands and knees, tugging Tracy down beside him. He gestured for her to wait there and then crawled up the sharp incline, past shale and granite outcroppings. Near the top he slipped the binocular strap over his head and clenched the glasses in one hand, and flattened out onto his stomach and inched up to a point just below the top, where he could see the bay and the whole of the cove behind it.

Propping himself up on his forearms, he steadied the glasses at his eyes. The beach and the greensward over by Jonas' cottage and the lawn before the house were deserted; the wooden cross stood smouldering—one of the charred arms had collapsed. Darkness shrouded all the windows in the house, filled the foyer beyond the still-open front door.

Jackman pushed himself backward, rolled over and skidded down to where Tracy was on heels and one palm. He told her what he had seen, and what he had not seen. "Maybe they're in the house," he said, "or out looking for us."

"Or with their boat," Tracy said.

"We'll take it slow and careful."

"Where do we look first?"

"Out at the end of the Neck. In the marsh."

"Where else can it be, if not there?"

"On the far side of the headland across the bay. There's a shallow inlet there where you could moor a small boat."

"No other place?"

"I don't think so."

"This is your goddamn island; don't you *know?*"

Inside the cowllike hood of her slicker, her face had the look of damp white clay, the eyes like dark holes deeply gouged out by the fingers of an angry sculptor. He knew she was fatigued from all the running and walking they had done, from the constant tension and fear; knew it because even though he was in good physical condition—he played handball whenever he could, jogged whenever he could—he felt the same way himself. No matter how good a shape you were in, you were never prepared for a situation like this: not physically and not mentally. His thoughts had a faint fuzziness at the edges now, the kind of fuzziness you experienced after having the one drink too many. You could still function well enough, but you could not quite trust your judgments or your emotional responses.

With a steadiness that even to him sounded forced, he

91

said, "Jonas has lived out here for nearly forty years, and according to him the bay and the east cove are the only two places you can land a boat. So it's not probable that it could be anywhere else. But I suppose it's possible; just about anything is possible, we both know that all too well."

She looked away from him, scrubbed at her face, looked back. More calmly, then, she said, "I'm sorry, David. Nerves. I'm scared shitless."

"We both are," he said, and caught her hand and helped her to her feet. "Let's just move one square at a time, all right?"

"All right."

They went seaward along the side of the Neck, into the perimeter of the marshland. The earth there was covered with night-grotesque forms: gnarled and stunted pines, flowering shad, bayberry and wild cranberry shrubs, thick patches of catalpa grass and high brown reeds. The croaking of frogs and the occasional screeching of gulls and egrets penetrated fog massed like thin layers of whipped cream or swirling sinuously in changing designs along the shore and out over the water. Their steps made liquid squishing sounds in the boggy ground.

It took them three or five or ten minutes to reach the tip of the peninsula; Jackman was not sure because his sense of time-perception seemed to be malfunctioning. But time did not mean anything now, except in relation to the coming dawn, and that was still at least three hours away.

They uncovered several duck nests and startled a small animal that was probably a muskrat, but they did not uncover any sign of a boat.

They crouched beside a sassafras bush, inside a misty swath of reeds. Water lapped over their ankles, and the footing beneath it was thick mud and slippery rock. Jackman tried to work spit through his dry mouth, but the saliva glands were desiccated. All the moisture in his body seemed to be leaking out through his pores: he felt as though he

92

were marinating in sweat. Much worse than that, the visceral tension was beginning to take its toll; his nerves had tightened to the danger point.

He drew several deep, silent breaths and stared out over the marsh. They had gone over no more than a sixth of it, but it was dotted toward the center with sinkholes and patches of mud as treacherous as quicksand. If the boat were hidden anywhere on this side of the Neck, it would have to have been brought in either in the vicinity of where they now were—in which case they should already have found it—or down near the line of evergreens, a less likely mooring or hiding place.

Jackman swiveled his gaze to the Neck's outer reaches. The land there was peaked into a tiny promontory, the base of which was strewn with seaweed-draped boulders and tide-covered mudflats; on the promontory and the rest of the higher ground atop the peninsula, projections and knobs of rock jutted up through the grass like warts and blemishes. There was nowhere at the tip, or near it on this side, where a boat could have been secreted. The only possible place was over on the bay side, just in from the breakwater, where a plot of tall sedges grew close to the sloping side.

The juxtaposition of the rocks at the foot of the point made it too difficult and too dangerous to go around that way. So he would have to head up across the promontory and then down in order to check the plot of sedges, and that meant crawling most of the way to avoid silhouetting himself against the sky.

He whispered all of this to Tracy. She did not want to be left alone again, that was obvious in the way she looked at him, the way her fingers clutched at his arm. But when he said, "It won't take long either way; you'll be able to see me most of the time from here," she nodded jerkily, held his arm a moment longer and then released it.

Jackman straightened and went around the bush, sliding his shoes gingerly through the water and the grasping mud.

When he had waded through a shock of catalpa grass he was on a hummock of dry, solid turf that connected with the side of the Neck. He could move more rapidly then, and he ran bent over across the hummock, onto the slope, up it toward where one of the larger knobs of rock canted skyward at the crest.

He had taken half a dozen steps when the man came out from below and behind the rock knob.

Jackman stopped as suddenly as if he had walked into a wall. He stared incredulously, and his stomach spasmed and turned over; he was unable to move, to react—suspended for a moment in time and space. The man was big, young, naked to the waist. On his chest, gleaming black in the moonlight, was the same cabalistic sign that had been drawn in blood on the cottage door, on the note attached to the fawn's bone. He held a rifle in both hands, but he stood as motionless as Jackman, matching his stare.

Fifty yards away to the right, a second armed and half-naked man appeared on top of the Neck.

It took a cry from Tracy below to release Jackman from paralysis. Panic climbed in him, shrieking mutely. He spun and stumbled downslope, across the hummock; water sprayed up around his ankles as his feet slashed through it and into the muck beneath. Tracy was running too: he could see her plunging away into the marsh. He fought his way through reeds and shrubs, altering his course toward hers, cutting around a stunt pine, avoiding at the last second a pool of muddy water that marked a boghole. Hammering pulse created a rage of sound in his ears; there was pain in his chest, pain in his groin where muscles had knotted.

He did not want to look back, he did not want to see how close the two men were behind him, but it was impossible to resist the need. And when he finally did pivot his head, he saw them still on the slope—coming down it to the marshland at a pace that seemed surprisingly unhurried, the rifles still held across their bodies rather than butted up at their shoulders in shooting position.

94

He twisted his head to the front again, and Tracy was just disappearing into a cloud of mist that appeared to cling hammocklike between two shad trees spaced thirty yards apart. A moment later he heard a crashing noise, a splash, the muffled plaint of her voice. He bulled through a chest-high swatch of reeds, came out in a wide clump of thistle; thorns stung at his legs below the hem of the oilskin.

When he neared the layer of fog he could still hear Tracy thrashing around somewhere within it. He swept through with his arms flailing and puffs of the mist rising like smoke, his eyes searching down low to the ground. He located her almost instantly: she was on her knees at the edge of a sink-hole, struggling to rise, her back to him. As soon as she heard him coming up behind her she lunged to her feet, staggered, fell again whimpering. He reached her, caught her arm, and she fought him blindly, frantically, nails flashing, until he said, "It's me, Ty, it's me!" and then she sagged into him, and he was able to hoist her upright. He pulled her forward and onto firmer ground, his legs churning awkwardly in the mud as he circled around trees and shrubs blurred by fog and by his own sweat-filmed eyes.

And while they ran, a sense of unreality bordering on farce came over him. An image of the two of them running danced through his mind: they must look ridiculous, stripped of all dignity. If only his fellows in Washington could see him now! Jackman the fool. Reductio ad absurdum. Jesus. . . .

Ahead, the land dipped and opened into a wide backwater pool, heavily verged with sedges and swamp grass. He hesitated at the edge of it. The shortest way to the concealing trees beyond was straight across the pool, and it looked shallow enough, safe enough to wade through without becoming mired—and acting on impulse, then, he took Tracy into the silt-heavy water.

It came up over their knees at first and the footing was good; but when they reached the center, mud slid away beneath his shoes and he went under, brackish water spilling into his open mouth, Tracy's hand sliding out of his: she had gone under too. He kicked up, broke surface and saw her floundering beside him, coughing. He caught hold of her, steadied her against him, and together they swam a few strokes clumsily. When he put his feet down again, the mud supported his weight, and he straightened himself and Tracy up in the waist-deep water and then plowed forward until it was shallow enough to allow them to run again.

The marsh growth was thinner on the opposite side, the earth less swampy. They sprinted through it toward the trees looming blackly ahead, and he knew they were going to get into them all right, get away without being caught. Looked back instinctively to confirm this and saw no sign of the two men in the foggy marsh behind them.

Then they were into the woods, and he cut a diagonal course to the left, inland, not slowing, half-dragging Tracy now because he could tell that her strength was nearly gone. His thoughts had begun to jumble, turn sluggish, but he understood the need to find sanctuary as soon as possible—a place to hide, to rest, to regain control. The fort? Yes, the circle of rocks where he and Dale had pretended to be New World Indians or adventurous explorers, where they had once played a grand hiding game for an entire day in retaliation for what they had considered an unjust punishment, and the Old Man and Charlie Pepper had not been able to find them. Loop through the forest behind the house, out to the point on the north shore and into the rock fort where these men could not find them either.

He understood something else, too: that the two men on the Neck could have caught them, could have used the rifles to wound them. And why hadn't they? Because they felt they were in control of this game, and ending it too soon, like ending any game too soon, would have lessened the ecstasy of a final triumph—the checkmate, the last out, the deathstroke?

Sweet Jesus God. . . .

SUNRISE.

Across a section of the rocky point on the north shore, and through a thin copse of trees, the sun appeared poised on the edge of the sea, glinting redly. The sky around it was streaked in diluted crimson, like bloody fingermarks. Early-morning sounds filled the cool air: the singing of land birds, the squawking of the ever-present gulls, the faint buzzing of bees and sand flies. Small black crabs skittered over the rocks; the sea glittered with reflections of light from the new sun.

On the westward, inner edge of the point, a rock overhang jutted out from a steep incline topped by pine and a single weathered oak. Beneath the overhang, sweeping out from it on the inland side, a cluster of craggy boulders and humps of granite six to eight feet high formed four-fifths of a rough circle; the other fifth was open to the sea but could not be seen from anywhere except directly out on the tip of the point. Within that circle was a small pocket: the fort of Jackman's youth.

He and Tracy sat there side by side on a bed of smooth pebbles and strips of seaweed, butted against one of the boulders. There was just enough room in the narrow enclosure for them to stretch their legs out full length. Her eyes were closed, and she seemed to be sleeping; but his eyes were wide, fixed. He sat rigidly with his hands gripping his knees beneath the open flaps of his slicker.

He was calm now and had been for some time, but it was a terrifying kind of calm; there was a primal scream buried just beneath the surface of it. His body ached, and he wanted desperately to sleep—sleep not only renewed strength, it solidified your grip on sanity. But he had not been able to

97

close his eyes for more than a few minutes since they had come to the fort. For the first hour they had held each other, not speaking because there was nothing to say in the dying hours of the night. After awhile, exhausted, she had drifted off into a fitful slumber; and he had simply sat there, watching the sky, waiting for dawn, hanging onto the calm and trying to force his thoughts to remain clear and systematic.

In the past few minutes a sense of overwhelming helplessness had taken hold of him. Every tactic, every potential move, seemed futile.

The boat. If it was in that plot of sedges on the inner curve of Eider Neck—and the presence of the two men there indicated that it probably was—there was no way to get to it, no way to avoid or neutralize the long-range threat of the rifles. There was still a remote possibility that the boat was hidden on the headland that formed the northwestern boundary of the bay; but the terrain there was too heavily wooded to be easily defensible. They were expert gamesmen too, they had proved that during the night: they would have planned their own strategy with intelligence and craft, like a military mission. (And *could* they be former army or marine personnel, as Tracy had half-suggested?)

A signal for help. They had nothing with which to signal a passing lobster or pleasure boat, or to alert anyone on the nearest inhabited island. Nothing, that was, except fire—and a fire big enough to command investigation had to be built either on the cliffs or here on the point, and then tended constantly to keep it burning bright enough to be seen at a distance; but it would also attract the attention of the opponents, bring them running to snuff it out and tell them just where he and Tracy were. Then there was the danger of sparks carrying on the shifting winds and igniting the forestland. He had seen a small island on fire once, and the rapidity with which it had been consumed was astonishing: burning trees sailing through the air like massive hurled faggots to torch off other trees, fire traveling along the interlocking

98

root structure beneath the surface of the earth, feeding on the inflammable sap of the pines and spruce. This entire island could turn into a raging inferno in a matter of hours—and while that would certainly drive the opponents away in their boat, it would also trap him and Tracy. There was nowhere they could go to escape it except into the caves at the foot of the cliffs, and they could only remain there as long as the tide was at ebb. If they were not found and rescued before flood tide, they would drown.

Mount some sort of offensive. They were two people armed with knives; the enemy was at least two and perhaps more, armed with handguns and rifles. A direct confrontation would be suicidal. Set some sort of traps? But what kind? Where? He had no tools and no time to dig pitfalls or fashion vine-triggered missiles or snares, no assurance even if he had that they would work. Jonas and the Old Man had taught him a little woodsman's lore, and he knew the island better than the opponents could ever know it; but what good was any of that except as a help in avoiding capture? It would not give them the upper hand, and it would not get them off the island.

Wait and hide and pray they would not be found. Jonas and his wife might come out on Tuesday when he didn't bring the cruiser back, but then again they might simply think he had decided to stay on and wait days or even a week before they considered something to be wrong and came to investigate. And even if they did show up, there was nothing to stop the enemy from killing them outright or capturing them and making them part of whatever blood rites were planned for him and Tracy. They had only the small amount of food she had taken from the kitchen and pantry last night, some of which had probably been lost or rendered inedible by submergence in the backwater pool in the marsh; and their chances of getting into the house for more were realistically zero. They could eat pine nuts and green berries, but without fresh water—and there was virtually none on the island this time of year except that piped into the house and cottage from an underground cistern—they could not last more than five or six days.

What would the Old Man, that Grand Master of Gamesman, have done in a situation like this? Jackman thought. In 1960, when he had apparently been defeated for reelection with 78 percent of the precincts reporting, he had said, "I will not concede defeat. I will not concede defeat until all the votes are in and I am behind, and even then I will demand a recount." And one of his aides, in Jackman's hearing, had said immediately to another aide, "And if the recount fails, he'll ask for another one and use every dime he's got to fix the results." That was the Old Man, all right: never give up, never say die, ruthlessly competitive to the very end because any game can be won no matter how enormous the odds—even one like this.

If you can stay in it, he thought. If you can keep from breaking down.

Beside him Tracy stirred and made a soft moaning sound. Then, suddenly and violently, her eyes popped open and she jerked away from the boulder and onto her knees, staring at him disconnectedly and with shining terror. He said her name, said it again, and awareness seeped into her and cleared her vision and dulled the terror. She sank back on one hip and lifted her head and breathed tremulously. Her face was pocked with scratches, pimpled red with insect bites, and the skin under her eyes and across her cheekbones had a puckered, waxy look; strands of hair, matted with dried mud, lay flat against her forehead and fell stiffly from inside the pulled-back hood of her slicker. She looked ten years older than she was, and he knew his own appearance was as bad or worse.

Compassion rose in him, and he touched her hand. She pulled it away from him, but impersonally, as if she could not bear to be touched by anyone. She put her spine against the boulder again and hugged herself, staring up at the coralline sky.

He said tentatively, "How do you feel?"

"Wonderful. Lovely. How do you think I feel?"

"Frightened," he said. "Like me."

"How reassuring for both of us."

"I'm just facing facts, Ty."

"So am I. And it's hopeless: we're dead."

"No. . . ."

"Dead, sitting here dead. Why didn't they kill us last night? They could have; they could have caught us in that marsh. At least it would be over now and we wouldn't have to keep on waiting for it to happen. That's worse than dying, David—the waiting for something you know is inevitable."

"It's not inevitable. We've still got a chance."

"What chance? We didn't find the boat, did we."

"It's got to be in that patch of sedges I told you about."

"Suppose it is. How do we get to it?"

"I'm not sure we can."

"Then we can't get off the island. And we can't fight them. What else is there?"

"Faith," he said.

"In what? God? Miracles?"

"In ourselves, in our ability to find a way to survive. There has to *be* a way, Ty; there's always a way to do anything, even what seems to be the impossible."

"Thank you, Reverend Billy Graham."

That made him angry for a reason he could not identify—and with the anger came the realization that through all that had happened last night, all the running and searching and hiding, he had not once felt the emotion of rage. He concentrated on it, and found it surprisingly good, assertive, a stabilizer for the brittle calm; it even helped to dissipate some of the feeling of helplessness, to give strength and credence to what had been little more than empty palliatives for Tracy's and his own fear. There *did* have to be a way. Somewhere in all those postulated negatives, there was a positive action and a positive result, he just had not found it yet.

"All right," he said, putting derision into his voice, "it's

101

hopeless, we're going to die, we're already dead. Then we might as well walk out of here right now and go back to the house and give ourselves over to them. Is that what you want? Give yourself up like a lamb for slaughter? Or do you want to fight for your life? Maybe you'll fail, maybe you will die, but does it make any sense not to fight at all?"

She looked at him for a long moment, as if startled by his vehemence, and then turned her head aside. In a soft dull voice she said, "What do you want to do? Just sit in here, hiding? They'd find us eventually, you know that."

He did not answer. Instead he stood up and peered over the boulder, satisfied himself of the absence of movement among the trees that flanked the point on both inland sides. There was very little breeze: the pine boughs barely stirred. The sun had climbed higher off the eastern horizon, modulating the sky's flush into a soft gold sheen, filling the woods with dusky shafts and patches of its light. The night chill was already fading from the air; in another hour it would be warm, and by midday the temperature would be in the high seventies.

When he turned back, Tracy was watching him. He opened the snaps on his oilskin, shrugged it off, then sat down again with it spread over his lap. He said, "The first thing we have to do is take inventory of what's left after that dunking in the marsh."

He began emptying the slicker pockets, and after a moment, silently, she took hers off and followed suit. They put everything on the pebbles between them, and what they had were the two kitchen knives, one flashlight—the other one had been lost; a key-open tin of Spam, a sealed package of cheddar cheese, two oranges, an apple that was no good because it had gotten sliced open by one of the knives and then been soaked in swamp water, a small sodden inesculent box of raisins, two bars of bitter chocolate; and the mud-caked binoculars that still hung from around his neck. He tried the flashlight, holding the round glass end against his palm, and it worked all right; the batteries had not been water-damaged. One of the binocular lenses had a hairline crack, but when he cleaned both lenses with saliva and then tested them by focusing on the evergreens above, he found that the crack did not impair magnification or clarity.

He picked up the orange and extended it to Tracy, but she shook her head. "I can't eat anything," she said. "I'd just throw it up again, the way my stomach feels."

Jackman nodded—he knew he could not eat anything either—and said, "Okay, we'll save the food for later." He gathered it up and returned it to the pockets of one slicker, along with the flashlight. Then he scooped away pebbles until he exposed damp earth, widened the holes, rolled both oilskins into a bundle and put them into the depression, and covered them over with more of the pebbles.

Tracy said, "What now?"

"I think we ought to go over what we know about those men."

"We don't know anything about them."

"Yes we do. Not much, maybe, but a little. We know to begin with that there are at least two of them—the two that were out on the Neck. The one who showed himself directly in front of me was clean-shaven. I didn't get a good look at the second one, but I had an impression of a beard. How clearly did you see that one?"

"Not very," she said. "I was just starting to run when he showed himself."

"The one you saw at the kitchen window *did* have a beard?"

"Yes. He was no more than five feet away, and he had his face pressed right up to the glass."

"So we're still not sure if there are more than two."

Heavily: "If there are, our chances are that much worse."

"Granted," Jackman said. "But they're going to have to watch the boat, if only from a distance, and they're going to have to watch the house and the cottage; they don't want us getting in to stock up on food and water. One of them could handle all that, but not very well. So if there are only two, I don't think they'd risk a lone hunter to look for us. I doubt if they'd send just one man in any case."

"Why not?"

"Because they can't know the island as well as I do, and they'd have to realize the possibility of an ambush. Whatever else they are, they're not stupid."

"Then all of them are somewhere around the house."

"At this stage of things, yes."

"Then where does that leave us?"

"With some freedom of movement, at least."

"What good is freedom of movement?" Tracy said. She pressed the heels of her hands against both temples, as though her head ached harshly. "Their boat is at the bay, they're at the bay, and we can't get to any of them because we don't know where any of them are."

"We should be able to find out whether or not the boat really is in those sedges."

"How?"

"By going out on the bay headland on this side. From there I can use the binoculars. The house and grounds will be visible from there too."

"But we still can't get to it or them—"

"One square at a time, remember?" Jackman said. The anger continued to energize him, provide him with the impetus for positive thinking and direction. "Once we learn exact locations, we can start worrying about what to do next. We can't accomplish anything as long as we're blind."

Her eyes held his. "You really believe there's hope."

"Yes. Damn it, yes."

"I guess that's enough for both of us, then," she said. Her mouth formed a wry, humorless smile. "The good guys always win, right? All they have to do is to hang in there and they'll come out on top."

"No," he said, "not always. But this time."

He stood again, and Tracy did the same in stiff, enervated movements. Watching her, he became conscious again of the aching in his own body: they must have run five miles or better during the night.

He said, "Maybe I'd better go alone to the headland. You'd be safe here and you could rest—"

"No. No way, Senator. I'm strong enough and I can keep fighting if you can, but not if I have to do any more waiting by myself. I'll revert to stereotype and go to pieces like a damned hysterical female unless we stay together."

Jackman understood that: she took strength from him, and perhaps the reverse was true as well. He nodded grimly.

She asked, "How far is it to the headland?"

"Less than a fifth of a mile."

"I can make that all right."

"We'll take our time," he said. "Later, we can come back here and try to sleep. No matter what we find out, there isn't anything we can do about it during the daylight hours. The only advantage we have is the cover of darkness."

THE SHALLOW INLET on the headland's outer, northward curve had ten-foot shale banks that rose steeply out of the placid sea. A dense stand of trees bordered it on the north; toward the bay, the evergreens were more thinly spaced, interspersed with birch and an occasional oak. The ground behind the inlet was clear, covered with meadow grass and wildflowers and a long mossy hump of rock which formed a natural stone bench.

The area was deserted.

Jackman and Tracy crossed through the grass from the north. They had taken thirty minutes or better to approach the inlet, creeping within the woods until they had gotten close enough for him to use the binoculars. The fact that neither the boat nor the enemy was there, as he had suspected would be the case, strengthened his conviction that the craft was hidden in those sedges on Eider Neck.

At the edge of the cleared space he raised the glasses again and peered south through the trees, but he could not see much: patches of sun-bright water, of the Neck. They moved forward toward the bay, weaving from tree to tree, keeping their bodies low to the ground. When they neared the side of the headland, the woods gave way to clumps of fern and high grass and sphagnum moss, and finally to bare rock that fell away in jagged inclines to the water. He knelt behind the trunk of a pine, felt Tracy do the same close behind him. From there he had an unobstructed view of the Neck several hundred yards straight across the open bay, of part of the cove where the house was. The configuration of the headland was such that it bellied outward to his left, and the vegetation there obscured the house itself and the other buildings.

He steadied his left arm against the trunk and focused the glasses on Eider Neck, found the tall brown sedges near the breakwater. Thickly matted, motionless in the calm air, they still seemed far away—and he could not find the boat or a break in the reeds where the boat might be.

Tracy said, "Is it there? Can you see it?"

"No. We're too far away; the glasses aren't powerful enough."

Silence.

And a new possibility struck him, sickeningly. Suppose the boat was a small outboard made of fiberglass or aluminum? Once they had landed on the island, they could have *carried* it out of the water and hidden it somewhere, anywhere, inland. Christ!

His nerves began to jangle again; he struggled to hold onto the calm. No, he thought, no, the boat *has* to be in those sedges. The two men had been on the Neck last night; why would they have been waiting there unless it was to guard the boat? It was there, all right: he would not let go of the conviction. It was a foundation, no matter how flimsy, from which they could work. Without that foundation, without knowledge of some of the rules the opponents had made up for this game, there was only blind and impotent groping: defeat.

Jackman moved the binoculars slowly over the Neck, pausing at each of the outcroppings and knobs of rock where a guard might conceal himself. He saw no one, no movement. Abruptly he straightened and caught Tracy's hand, and they went laterally to the left and out to where the headland bellied, through the trees there until he had a full view of the closed boathouse, the beach, the three buildings. Again he swung the glasses in a slow arc, left to right, right to left. Stillness. Except for the charred cross standing obscenely on the lawn, the faint reddish smears visible on the front of the cottage, everything appeared just as it had on their arrival yesterday afternoon.

"Anything?" Tracy said.

"No."

"So we haven't gained a thing coming out here," emptily.

"We've got the whole day ahead of us," he said. "There's no reason why we can't stay here, watching, instead of going back to the fort. One of them has to show himself sooner or later."

"All right," and she sank down onto the pine needles and crossed her arms on her knees and laid her head on them.

Jackman sat beside her and lifted the glasses once more to his eyes. . . .

CHAINS OF SECONDS.

Chains of minutes.

One hour, two hours, three hours.

The blue of the water, the green and brown of the trees, the white of the cobble beach, the yellow of the sunlight—all of it photograph-still. But once in a while the images and the colors blurred together, soft focus, dissolving—

His body spasmed and his head came up and he shook it rapidly, blinking to clear his vision: he had nearly fallen asleep again. He was lying on his stomach, propped up on his forearms; he shifted position until he was sitting on his right hip, and rubbed at the gritty mucus that filmed both eyes. He had already dozed off twice, once for what might have been several minutes. The air was warm, the cushion of pine needles soft beneath his body, and lassitude had seeped into every space of him.

The hands on his watch indicated that it was twenty past one. Lifting the binoculars for the fiftieth or the hundredth time, he moved them through what had by now become an habitual ninety-degree arc, from the cottage around to the tip of Eider Neck. And for the fiftieth or the hundredth time, he saw the same familiar sights and the same desertion.

Two hours or so earlier, he had thought he discerned movement at one of the house's upstairs front windows. But his perception of it as he panned with the glasses had been so brief, so indistinct at the corner of sight that it was virtually subliminal; and when he had snapped the binoculars back and held them on the window, there was nothing to see. Still, it had been the one in his old room: they could have been taking turns sleeping in there. That would at least partly explain why he had seen no indication of anyone in the past three hours. Spending the day inside the house, watching, feeding vicariously on the frustrations and fears of their quarry; waiting for nightfall, maybe, before they came out again. Creatures of the night, worshipers of Darkness, shadow predators.

But were they really that confident of winning with a minimum of struggle? That unconcerned with the danger of outside intervention? Young men who had lived through the horrors of war, who had adopted a different type of horror as their irreligion, might well be both of these things. Or was there more to it than that—something about the rules of this game that he did not quite understand as yet . . . ?

"You'd better let me take the glasses for a while, David," Tracy's dulled voice said behind him. "You look ready to pass out."

It startled him, jerked his head around: the last time he had checked on her, she had been asleep, curled foetally at the base of a balsam spruce. Now she was sitting up against the bole, watching him. There was color in her cheeks and she appeared rested and alert.

Jackman dry-washed his face, palms scraping audibly across the beard stubble on his cheeks. He did not want to give in to the fatigue, but he would not have a choice pretty soon; he would sleep before long either way, and it would benefit him more if he gave in to it willingly. Tracy could do a far more attentive job of keeping a vigil than he could now.

He said, "Okay, you're right," in a voice that sounded thick, faintly hollow, and took the binoculars from around his neck and gave them to her when she crawled over beside him. Their eyes met, held, shifted apart. She knew he had seen nothing, and he knew she knew it, and there was nothing for either of them to say. He watched her fit the glasses to her eyes, fiddle with the focusing knobs, hold steady in the direction of the house, then begin to scan. When she was looking out toward the end of Eider Neck, without having spoken, he rolled over onto his stomach and put his head in the fold of his arms and closed his eyes.

But sleep did not come immediately, in spite of his exhaustion. Instead his mind drifted, in and out of thought patterns, in and out of nooks and crannies of memory; then, like a roulette ball settling finally into a slot, his consciousness focused on a single memory, forgotten, hidden away, resurrected at this time and place for reasons known only to his psyche: the summer of his fourteenth year, and the girl named Linda Fong who had come into his life then. . . .

Linda Fong is the daughter of the live-in cook the Old Man has hired out of Bangor, and she is one year older than he is—old enough to wear a maid's costume and to help with the cleaning and serving at the parties. She is also a beautiful girl, with huge black eyes, and he is enchanted by her. They become friends, and he shows her the island, shows her the fort and the other special places, and they talk about many things and discover they have many of the same interests and attitudes. She is the happiest person he has ever known, always smiling, and when she laughs, which is often, her eyes sparkle and a dimple appears in her right cheek.

One evening toward the end of summer, the Old Man gives an old-fashioned fish fry. Hoop nets are set out in the bay to catch sculpin and flounder, and there are bonfires along the beach and lanterns hanging from the ornate ground poles, and buffet tables laden with salads and ears of sweet Maine corn and fat tomatoes and home-baked bread and blueberries in sugared cream, and fifty or sixty guests and half a dozen servants and the three-piece band from Milbridge. Linda is supposed to help, but that afternoon he takes her to explore the caves at the bottom of the cliffs and they lose track of time and it is almost dusk before they realize it. They run back through the woods, holding hands— her hand is warm and soft in his and he feels very good even though he is worried about keeping her out so long—and when they reach Eider Neck he sees that most of the guests are already there on the beach. Linda is apprehensive and wants to go directly to her room in the house to change clothes, but he pulls her with him toward the beach because

110

he wants to explain to his father that it is his fault she is late, and because he wants to ask that she be relieved of her duties tonight so she can join him for the fish fry.

When they run in among the guests, hands clasped, activity stops and people stare and begin to murmur, he does not know why, and his father appears looking angry and sends Linda away, harsh-voiced. Then the Old Man takes him aside and asks him what he thinks he's doing, and he says he does not understand, and the Old Man says, "She's *Chinese*, boy," and he says, "What difference does that make?" and the Old Man says, "It makes all the difference in the world when you come running here holding her hand like she was white," and the next day Jonas takes Linda and her father away from the island and he never sees her again.

But the following week the Old Man invites a congressman, Fred Tremaine, to visit the island for a few days, and when Tremaine arrives he has his daughter with him. Her name is Judy and she is the same age as he is, and pretty— but not as pretty as Linda—and has large breasts and corn-colored hair. During their stay he takes Judy exploring, as he took Linda, but it is not the same, she giggles too much and smokes cigarettes from a package she hides in her purse. On the last night she asks him to take a walk with her and they go into the woods and she maneuvers him into a quiet little glade and before long they are sitting down and she is kissing him, putting his hand on her breast, urging him to open her blouse and take off her bra, and after he has done that she pushes him down on the soft pine needles and touches his erection, rubs it, and says Take it out, Davey, I want to hold it, and he does that and she grasps it and while he fondles her breasts she masturbates him until he comes into her lace handkerchief—and the next morning, as Judy and her father are preparing to leave for the mainland, the Old Man takes him aside again and says, "Now *she's* the kind of girl you should be running with, son, she's one of your own. . . ."

Jackman shifted position, and the memory was gone as

quickly as it had come. Threads of sleep finally dulled his thoughts, but it was that kind of thin, fitful, oppressive sleep which never quite blocks out awareness. Sounds penetrated—Tracy moving nearby, the song of a blackbird, something scurrying—and then faded to silence, and then returned again in an almost rhythmic cycle. He dreamed, and as always a part of him seemed to stand off at a distance and observe the images flickering back and forth on the screen of his mind.

There was no sequence to the dream or dreams; there was only a disquieting jumble of fragments—a patchwork nightmare. A squirrel sitting on a pine bough, chattering, its belly cut open and blood leaking from the wound. Alicia screaming at him, "I'm going to kill myself, David, I mean it!" and then drawing the sharp blade of a knife across her throat. The Old Man talking, mouth moving at twice the normal speed but with no words coming out. The little Vietnamese boy with the blood all over his face, hiding his face. A half-naked man holding a giant gun, flames leaping and flaring around him and on his chest a symbol of black-magic that glistened red and undulated like a live thing, sensual in its caresses. The Old Man again, mouth still moving too fast, but now his words audible in a kind of Donald Duck chatter: *game plan, great game, man's game, chess game, fair game, all a game game game game. . . .*

The dreams stopped altogether, and there was a void.

And out of the void, a long while later, the face of Jonas and Jonas' gruff Down East voice: "Ayuh, I undertook to sell the *Carrie B* couple months back, Mr. Jackman. Fella from Milbridge offered me a good price, and me gettin too old to go lobsterin much these days, w'a'nt a heft of sense in lettin her sit in drydock most of the year. Fella didn't want my pots and buoys, nor anything else off her, and I ain't got a place here on the Main to store 'em. So put nigh everything in the barn out on the island, hope you don't mind."

Pots and buoys. Boys and pot. Sons and guns, leaps and flares—

Jackman woke up.

He lay for a second, then lifted onto hands and knees, dimly saw slanting rays from the sun tilted westward in a hazy, late-afternoon sky. *Pots and buoys.* The dream still had hold of him, he could still hear Jonas' voice echoing in his mind: a voice from three summers ago, the summer Jonas had sold the lobster boat he'd owned for thirty-five years, the summer of Meg's last visit to the island. And later that same day . . . later, on the island, he had gone out to the barn and rummaged through the stored goods from the *Carrie B*—a nostalgia trip, a reaching back through the past to touch a tangible part of those cold morning hours before dawn when he and Dale and Jonas had gone out to run the string of lobster traps. *Pots and buoys.* And among them, *sons and guns,* among them, *leaps and flares,* among them—

Flare gun, the emergency flare gun!

Jackman reared up on his knees, did not feel the painful protest in sleep-stiffened joints or the parched soreness in his throat. The dream released him, but there was no feeling of grogginess; instead his thoughts were sharp, and he had a vivid image of the flare pistol as he had seen it—flares, too, half a dozen of them—in a box of miscellaneous goods three years ago. The memory had been buried in his subconscious, and it had taken the random association of his dreams to drag it out; there had been too much strain and too much tension for his conscious mind to have recalled it unaided.

Emotion flooded through him: excitement, fresh hope, resolution. He looked for Tracy, saw her sitting cross-legged beside one of the trees, scanning the cove and Eider Neck with the glasses. When he said her name she turned, shoulders slumped, and moved her head from side to side in a defeated way and started to speak—and then became aware of his expression and frowned questioningly as he came over to her, gripped her arms.

He told her about the flare gun.

She stared at him as if she could not quite believe what he

was saying, as if she did not dare to believe it. "David," she said finally, "David, are you *sure?*"

"I'm sure it was there three years ago."

"Three years is a long time—"

"Jonas wouldn't have removed it. He's never bought another boat, and the cruiser had its own emergency pistol."

"But those freaks could have searched the barn, found it—"

"No. No. That collection of guns in my father's study contained a dozen different types of firearm. They would have thought every gun on the island was stored there. They probably searched the cottage, yes; but there wouldn't have been any reason for them to suspect anything was in the barn. It's still there, Ty—and we can get to it. Wherever they are, whatever they're watching for, the barn should be the last place they expect us to go."

She kept on looking at him, and he could see some of the same emotions which filled him slowly seeping into her. "If we can, if the pistol is still there, then what?"

Jackman's mind raced, plotting, calculating: the gamesman in him had been regenerated. "We'll take it to the fort," he said. "There are plenty of boats in this area, pleasure craft, lobster fishermen, trawlers; as soon as we spot one, tonight or tomorrow, we'll fire a flare. They'll respond out of curiosity, if nothing else. When they do we'll swim out and let them pick us up."

"What if *they* see it too?"

"They won't; we'll shoot at a low trajectory. And a flare gun is also a weapon, don't forget that."

Tracy said, "God, maybe . . . maybe . . . " and leaned against him, and they sat there hanging onto each other and this new hope in the warmth of the lowering sun.

114

THEY CAME BACK to the fort a half hour before sunset.

Long shadows stretched through the pine woods and the trees looked black against the variegated backdrop of the sky. The sea had a burnished sheen. A light northerly wind had begun drawing, tinged with coldness, and it fanned their faces as they came out onto the point, slipped around and through, into the small pocket within the rocks.

Jackman sank to his knees and scraped away the pebbles covering the buried slickers. He unrolled the oilskins, took out one of the oranges and the wedge of cheese and a chocolate bar. Peeled the fruit and broke it into halves and gave one to Tracy. The juice soothed away some of the dryness in his throat, and he ate cheese and chocolate ravenously: with hope had come hunger. Tracy had difficulty getting the food down, but she managed to swallow all of it and keep it on her stomach.

Sitting on the headland, they had planned their strategy for tonight. They would wait, first of all, until after dark—but not too long after dark; there was nothing to be gained by holding off until the hours between midnight and dawn, and the waiting would be bad enough without extending it an additional five or six hours. There was no less a risk at three A.M. than there was at ten P.M. Once you were sure of your moves, you had to make them boldly, without hesitation, without worrying about contingencies: another of the Old Man's game-playing maxims.

Then they would circle around to the trees on the slope behind the barn, both of them together because Tracy was determined not to let him go alone, not wait by herself in the darkness. Come down out of the trees and cross perhaps sixty yards of open ground to the rear wall of the barn. There would be another full moon, and the sky was cloudless and looked as though it would remain that way; but even if one of the enemy was stationed on the rear porch of the house, or at an upstairs window, the barn would block off his view of the open ground. And once they made their way around to its front, the two leafy apple trees would act as a screen between the house and the barn, and provide concealing shadows as well.

After they were inside, Tracy would stand watch at the doors while he located the pistol and the flares; that way, they would have at least some insurance that when they went out they would not walk into an ambush. If he could locate the objects immediately, they would have to stay inside the barn no more than ten minutes, perhaps even as few as five. Then they would come directly back into the trees and return here to the fort.

It was a simple plan, and it would work; he refused to consider any of the things that could go wrong. Still, his nerves were thrumming again, and he seemed to have lost the excitement that had flooded him when he first remembered the flare pistol. He was unable to summon it again, or the anger or any of the other emotions. These would come later, he told himself, when the time arrived for them to put the maneuver into action. Meanwhile, there was nothing to do except to keep a tight grip on himself and try not to think—just what a soldier was taught to do before entering combat in that other mad game of war.

Tracy shifted beside him, seeking a less uncomfortable position on the bed of pebbles. She said, "What time is it?"

He glanced at his watch. "Seven-forty."

"Two hours."

"Yes."

"I wish I could sleep it away."

"Maybe you can."

"No way."

"Try closing your eyes."

116

She said nothing, and after a moment he looked over at her. Her eyes were closed. She held her hands fisted on her thighs, breathing audibly through her mouth. In the fading daylight her cheeks looked hollow, the skin of her face stretched thin and oddly translucent; the bone structure seemed so prominent that it was like a skull over which thin plastic had been molded to simulate human features. Jackman turned his head away, tilted it back against the boulder and stared up at the sky.

Time passed—so slowly that he came to imagine the ticking of a faulty clock, one tick every five or ten seconds. The last of the sunset hues disappeared from the western horizon—violet and old rose tonight—and the gray-black of encroaching darkness settled down. Cold stars appeared, and light from the moon that he could not quite see laid a faint whitish glow across the night. The air cooled more quickly and the wind grew stronger; the sea made whispering sounds, like a thousand muted voices heard from a vast distance.

And all the while gulls wheeled and dived out of sight and appeared again overhead in continuous patterns, their calls querulous and irritable and hungry: the vultures of the sea looking down on him and on Tracy as though resentful of the fact that they were still alive.

10:25.

In the perimeter of the woods behind the barn Jackman rested on one knee and moved the binoculars slowly from side to side. Tracy stood to his left, behind the canted trunk of a dead pine. Both of them wore the black oilskins again, the hoods drawn up to cover their heads.

They had been there for ten minutes, and there had not been anything to see or hear. No lights showed in the house, or anywhere else. Another low ground fog had started to flow in, but it was thinner, wispier than it had been last night. The random tendrils had the look of smoke in the polished-silver shine of the moon.

Jackman dropped the glasses to his chest, straightened up and touched Tracy's arm. "No point in waiting any longer," he murmured. "We'd better get it over with."

She looked at him silently for a moment, as if gathering her courage, and then released a soft sibilant breath. "I guess I'm as ready as I'll ever be," she said.

She stepped behind him and took hold of his slicker, and they went forward cautiously, keeping to the heavier pockets of darkness. When they left the last of the trees they hunched over as one and ran in awkward, shuffling, crablike strides toward the rear barn wall. Wind-blown leaves dotted the open ground and made soft crunching sounds under their feet; hidden twigs snapped twice, sounds that seemed to Jackman as loud as gunshots. He kept his head up and his eyes darting from one direction to another, and it seemed to him that they were running in slow motion, that it was taking an incredibly long time to cross those sixty open yards—the same sensations he had had when they fled the house almost twenty-four hours before. There was feeling in him now, as he had known there would be, but fear and rebuilding tension threatened to dominate; panic scuttled beneath the surface, and his face felt hot and swollen. He had to force his mind to remain blank.

Then, as though in a single enormous stride, they were at the southern corner of the barn. He leaned back against the boarding and took several breaths, took a solid hold on himself before he started forward again.

When they neared the front corner he could see more of

the area along the south side of the house, more of the space between the barn and the back of the house. The night seemed unnaturally still—no bird calls, no insect sounds; the sea not whispering in the distance. He stood motionless, straining to hear: something, anything. And a frog croaked somewhere behind them, two crickets serenaded each other in the grass, a mosquito buzzed his left ear, and suddenly he could hear the sea again, too, purling as it always did when the wind was up. All right. A momentary trick of perception. All right.

He eased his head out around the corner and looked diagonally across the front of the barn. The rear house door, visible between the trunks of the apple trees, was closed; shards of glass in the broken porch window gleamed dully. The upstairs windows were partially obscured by the branches, but he could see enough of them to tell that they were all like blind black eyes. Gusts of wind ruffled the leaves and the ferns growing over and along the rock retaining wall, bent the high grass on the lower section of the slope. Moonlight and shadow—and all of it fixed, empty, silent.

He looked at the barn doors, and they were still latched, as he and Tracy had left them last evening. It would take them no more than ten seconds to cross the half-dozen steps to the doors, open them, slip inside.

Jackman made one last reconnaissance of the area, held a breath, and made the run with Tracy still hanging tightly to his oilskin. His hand shook a little when he caught onto the latch, but he managed to get it open and himself through the parted halves without making excess noise. As soon as Tracy followed him in, he turned and pushed the doors closed to a slit and stood there listening.

To silence, except for the low vibratory hum of the generator.

Sweat trickled into his eyes and he wiped it away with the back of one hand. The darkness inside the barn was stygian; he could make out nothing except inchoate masses when he pivoted and let Tracy take his place at the doors. He lifted the flashlight from his pocket, then the handkerchief he had put in there with it earlier. When he had wrapped the cloth over the glass he touched the switch and the filtered light spread out fuzzily, bright enough for him to make his search but not, if he were careful, bright enough to penetrate the random chinks in the wall boarding.

He held the flash steady, aiming it straight ahead and angled slightly downward. There were no obstructions in the path to where the lobster traps and marker buoys and boxes of fishing gear were stacked behind the carriage. The carriage itself had a supernatural aura in the blurred light, as if he were looking through time to another era.

He started deeper into the barn. The flashlight beam cut away more of the blackness ahead, letting him see the workbench and the drill press and the piles of discarded furniture. He went along the left side of the carriage and stepped around an old hand lawnmower, up to the neat group of lobstering goods.

Beside the stack of curve-topped pots and the squared rows of red-and-white buoys were two rusting washboards and a coil of potwarp line and half a dozen rusted snatch blocks and a pile of folded seine nets for catching sardines; he did not immediately see the carton he remembered from three years ago. He leaned forward, sweeping the light, and there it was, behind one of the trap stacks. He knelt beside it, directed the beam inside and rummaged through the contents.

The flare pistol and the flares were not there.

He felt control begin to slip; each inhalation of air took on a hot-smoke feel in his lungs. They *had* to be there, Jesus they had to! His free hand scrabbled through the carton again, located a tackle box, fumbled it open: it contained tackle and nothing else.

Another carton, he must have overlooked it—and he stood and brought the light over the stacks, probing behind them, on both sides of them. There was no other carton, there was nothing, nothing, and the sweat drenched him now and his face felt swollen again and the primal scream that had underlain his thoughts that morning rose close to the surface. Think! Could Jonas have moved them for some reason, put them somewhere else in here? The workbench. A drawer in the workbench, that made sense, and he turned and started to swing the light around with him—

And Tracy cried out.

Shrieked, shrieked in sudden terror.

The stillness seemed to shatter around him like an impacted sheet of ice, slivers of it stinging cold against the back of his neck as the scream reverberated through the dark barn. He wheeled full toward the doors, the light swirling, and the two halves were parted wide now and he saw her silhouetted there in the opening, body turned toward him, struggling wildly because there was an arm around her neck and the half-naked shape of a man behind her, and she screamed again and clawed at the arm, face contorted in a ghastly rictus, and he stared in stunned unbelief as the arm and the shadow heaved her backward off her feet and out through the doors and she was gone, they were gone, and in their place another man-shape appeared briefly and then the doors slammed shut.

Christ God my God! and he was lunging along the side of the carriage, and in the night without Tracy shrieked again, half a scream this time that sliced off in mid-octave just as his foot twisted against something, and he lost his balance and sprawled down, pain searing over his upper ribcage, the flashlight jarring loose and spinning tracers of light that brightened as the handkerchief fluttered loose. He lurched up to his knees, to his feet, and saw that the flash had stopped spinning and the beam had steadied into an elongated shaft centered on the old top-coil icebox, and he staggered to where it lay and caught it up and kept on staggering to the doors, not thinking, not able to think, still hearing

Tracy's cries, and hit the doors full on with his right shoulder, expecting them to bounce open, but instead he caromed off and spun to one side, down to his knees again, when they bowed outward but did not part. He wagged his head, not comprehending, and gained his feet and hit the doors a second time, and again the latch failed to yield, the doors were *locked,* they had been locked somehow, and he dropped the flash and clawed at them, tearing his nails, screaming himself now, low in his throat, a sound that was not quite human.

Outside, there was only stillness.

When the moans in his throat strangulated into sharp gasping coughs, he stopped clawing at the doors and spun around with his hands spread out against them. At his feet the flashlight still burned, a harsh yellow strip laid across the black floor; a part of his mind registered this and he bent reflexively and picked it up. But then he did nothing except stand there holding the torch, trembling, disoriented, incapable of action or reason.

He said her name, "Tracy," he said, and the one word came out as a coughing sob.

Seconds went by—five, ten—and then his stomach convulsed and he retched emptily and that brought him out of it. Horror surged against the surface of his mind like surf against bare rock.

Get out of here!

He began to jerk his gaze and the light back and forth in rapid, frantic motions. Shadows and shapes leaped at him and receded again into walls of darkness. The gamesman in him was totally submerged; he had been reduced to atavism: a trapped animal seeking survival only through escape.

GET OUT OF HERE!

But there were no windows, no other doors, there was no way out except to go through those doors or through the walls, you couldn't walk through solid objects; the shaft of light still swinging back and forth, back and forth, low arc, high arc, the carriage, the stack of lumber, the roofing material, the bench saw, the furniture, the generator, the cordwood, the workbench, the tools hanging inside their painted outlines, the—

Tools.

Ax. Big double-bitted woodsman's ax.

And he put the light back on the wall above the workbench, probing for the ax, the ax should be there, Jonas using it during those summers long ago, using it himself: "Hey, Dad, did you see the way I felled that tree, just like a real lumberjack!" But it wasn't there, the ax was not there, and he ran to the bench and stabbed at the wall with the beam and found hammers, saws, screwdrivers, wrenches, but no ax, not even a hatchet, gone, all gone, and he pivoted away from the bench again, tears and sweat streaming from and into his eyes, half blinding him. He pawed his vision clear, *get out of here!* and ran along that wall, arcing the light, looking for something, anything that would mean a way out, and went past the lobstering gear and across the rows of cordwood and up the south wall, breathing torturedly, the primal scream rising again like bile into the back of his throat.

Nothing, nothing, and he made another circuit, big beast running around and around in a snare, and when he came back along the south wall this time his foot struck one of the plywood sheets and he stopped and shone the flash on the pile of lumber, the pile of lumber—six-foot length of four-by-four that had been left over when the barn was built.

Battering ram.

Immediately he leaned down and hefted the piece of

heavy wood and struggled with it to the locked doors. Put the flashlight into the pocket of his slicker, leaving it on, and got a solid two-handed grip on the timber and lunged at the doors. The four-by-four struck off-center on one half, sending echoes of sound through the barn, running splinters into his palms as it recoiled back against his stomach; the doors held. He made another run, and again struck off-center, and the understanding penetrated that he needed the light in order to see his target, the juncture of the two halves where the latch was.

He dropped the length of wood and got the flash out again and located a spindly felt-topped card table among the piled furniture. Carried that over to one side and laid the torch on top of it, positioned it so that the beam held fast on the doors at waist level. Then he stumbled back to the four-by-four and caught it up and made a third run at the doors, aiming at the latch, hitting the joining of the halves a little high. They bowed out, admitting a thin strip of moonlight between them, but still the locking device held them secured.

He made another futile run.

Another.

Another.

His hands were quilled with splinters now, slick with blood, and each time he drove the length of wood against the doors, pain shot up both arms and burst hotly across his chest. He could not get enough air into his lungs; muscles pinched and knotted all through his body; his legs threatened to cave in under him.

Another run.

This time, though the doors still held, there was the squealing sound of metal pulling free of wood.

He staggered back with the four-by-four and put his head down, panting, clinging to the timber with his bloody hands, and ran full speed at the doors, put all his weight behind the thrust. The square end of the wood hit dead center where the latch was, and he felt the other end slam back into his stomach and take away what breath he had been able to draw—

And then he felt it yield.

The doors flew apart, metal screeching, flying outward: a heavy bolt wedged through the padlock hasps that had been fastened to each half.

His momentum carried him through and sent him sprawling atop the four-by-four, then over it to a skidding halt in the wet grass fronting the barn. He tried to rise immediately, but he had no strength left in his arms and he could not breathe. His body flopped, his mouth open wide in silent gasps, as his lungs sought desperately to fill. Pressure built inside his head; he came close to blacking out.

Then both lungs heaved and air spilled in and he began to breathe again so rapidly, so painfully that his body seemed to throb up and down in a caricature of the motions of love-making. Strength flowed back into his arms, and he was able to pull himself onto all fours, and all at once he realized where he was and thought, *I did it, I'm out*—and a semblance of sanity returned to him.

He shoved onto his knees and then into a swaying upright position, cleansed his eyes with the back of one blood-smeared hand. He looked to the left, to the right, saw no one, nothing, and focused on the house beyond the screening branches of the apple trees.

The back door was open and there were lights on inside.

No, he thought, oh no, no.

Tracy, he thought.

Run, he thought, they're inside, waiting.

Tracy, he thought.

No. Run, run while you can.

Tracy, Tracy, Tracy. . . .

He groped in the oilskin's left pocket and got the knife out and started spasmodically toward the house. *No, run, into the woods!* and kept on going in a loose shambling walk past the apple trees and around the rock retaining wall, the knife held out in front of him like a short flat spear.

When he reached the open door, the scream tried to break out of him; he fought it back, lurched through and onto the porch. It was empty. The broken window glass glinted in the glare from the naked ceiling bulbs; the bloody animal leg still lay against the inner wall.

Just a game, all a game, only a game.

Run!

Tracy.

He went forward into the pantry, soft steps, listening: the house was still, a different kind of stillness from ever before, oppressive and threaded with menace. Into the kitchen, crouching. Lights burned here too, shining fixtures, gleaming linoleum, no sign or feeling of occupancy.

Across to the center corridor. Again he could not seem to take enough air; his breathing came in little choking pants, like the prelude to vomiting. His bladder felt suddenly, achingly bloated and the need to urinate was intense.

Into the center hall. Lightless—but beyond, in the parlor, there was a pale shimmering flicker of illumination. He stopped, heard silence like that in a vacuum: a total absence of sound. Chills capered the length of his body. Don't go in there. Run, Jesus Mary Mother, don't go in there! He tried to make himself back up, make himself turn, but his legs carried him instead to the archway, to where he could look into the parlor.

He could not see the source of the flickering light; it was coming from somewhere along the inner wall, where the fireplace was. He stood for a long moment, shaking, not wanting to go through the archway, knowing he would—Tracy—and then he caught the edge of the wall and propelled himself into the parlor, ten steps inside before he turned and looked at the fireplace.

Candles, six of them, burned atop the mantelpiece; another six flamed along the inner rim of the hearth. Pagan votives on a makeshift altar. And on the rest of the hearth bricks—

Splashes and puddles and streaks of liquid glistening blackly in the wavering light.

Blood.

Your blood next for the cup of Lucifer. . . .

Jackman began to shake his head. He stood shaking it faster and faster, until the candle flames became a single pale smear on the darkness. Then, abruptly, he quit that and made a whimpering sound and began backing away along the middle of the room, toward the foyer, and RUN! and he ran—into the foyer, kicked the table going by and sent the tape recorder sliding off it to bang and clatter on the floor. Got the door open and hurled himself through it onto the veranda and missed the top step and skidded down the rest of the stairs to land on one hip at the foot of them. He blinked his eyes free of wetness, started up.

Froze.

Twenty yards away on the lawn, not far from the remains of the charred cross, something stood outlined against the moonlit sky, something fluttered wispily in the cold night wind.

A pole, driven into the turf; and atop it

No

On top of the pole

No

Shining white, shining blood-black

And the fluttering was her hair

Tracy's hair

They they they had cut off her her

He screamed. And kept on screaming as he came up in one motion and ran away from the thing on the lawn, away into darkness that was now both the island and the inclosure of his mind.

PART THREE

Sunday, May 24:
THE ISLAND

*Whoever battles with monsters had better see that it does not turn him into a
monster. And if you gaze long into an abyss, the abyss will gaze back at you.*

—NIETZSCHE "Aphorisms and Entr'actes," *Beyond Good and Evil*

BLIND FLIGHT. . . .

Jackman did not know where he was or where he was going, he did not see or feel the tree branches like long-nailed fingers reach for his face and scrape thin furrows in the skin, he did not hear the whimpering explosions of his breath. When something caught his foot and sent him sprawling, he got up immediately and had no awareness of having fallen. Inside his head thoughts swirled in a red-tinged intermix, without coherence or continuity, like bits of flotsam tossing on a nightmare sea.

A stitch in his side impeded his breathing finally, made him slow to a lurching stagger. His hands clawed the air in front of him; then his knees buckled and he fell sideways against a down log, cracked his head with enough force for the pain to register and momentarily blank his mind. He tried to rise, could not. He pulled his knees up to his chest and curled himself and wrapped his arms over his head.

Then he began to tremble, and his body shook with such force that a fantasy thought penetrated: he was going to shake himself apart, limbs and organs and bones would frag-

131

ment like the atoms in a dropped figurine and there would be nothing left of him but scattered shards. He covered his head more tightly, pressed his knees harder against his chest. But he could not stop the quaking—

And he had a sudden sensation of falling, of diminishing in size and turning over and over inside himself and then fracturing, arm coming off and sailing away, a leg, his genitals, his head—and the head shrieked soundlessly and disappeared into a crimson tide that dissolved instantly into black.

Black.

When he came out of it, or seemed to come out of it, he was no longer trembling and his head felt clear—until he sat up and looked around him. Drooping evergreen boughs, thick trunks hung with moss, lacy webs of luminous mist . . . but all of it was distorted, grotesque, like a piece of forest seen through the bottom of a dark glass bowl.

'Twas brillig, and the slithy toves/Did gyre and gimbel in the wabe. . . .

Delirium.

Oh my God, don't let me break down!

All mimsy were the borogroves. . . .

He shut his eyes, but when he opened them again the distortion remained. And he remembered sitting with Dale during one of those long-ago summers, alone together in Dale's room, all the lights out, telling ghost stories, and Dale saying, "Have you ever thought what it might be like if you got locked up in one of your dreams? I mean, if you couldn't escape the dreamworld by waking up, and you had to spend the rest of your life walking around in it, trying to avoid the things that live there in the shadows?"

Cold encased his body; moisture leaked out of his pores and seemed to crystallize rather than flow wetly. He jammed the heels of his hands against his temples, twisted his head within them. But the warped boughs appeared to droop lower, swaying at odd menacing angles in a wind that did not whisper or sigh but made a sound in his ears like the crinkling of cellophane. Limbs seemed to reach malevolently, like bony fingers. Or claws. Or jaws.

Beware the Jabberwock, my son! The jaws that bite, the claws that catch!

He flung himself onto his stomach, hands digging at the soft damp needle humus. But as soon as he closed his eyes this time, he was back in Saigon and the plastique bomb had just exploded. He ran up the smoky, sweltering street, shouting and screaming on all sides, people lying shattered, and saw the boy with blood all over him and knelt beside him and began to brush away the blood pumping bright sticky red, and when the blood was cleared off, the face he saw belonged to Tracy—

He popped his eyes open again. Looked up.

Tracy's head floated above him on a red-smeared cloud, mouth open wide and accusing, strands of midnight hair fanned out in the crinkling-cellophane wind and glowing with a bluish radiance.

A cry burst out of him and he crawled away behind a tree and buried his head in his arms. Tracy, I'm sorry, I'm sorry! The name of the game is horror, and I don't know how to play. They're going to get *my* head too, *my* blood for the cup of Lucifer. . . .

The ground beneath him seemed to begin undulating, as though he were being rocked in a giant cradle. Voices screamed in the night around him: the burbling of Jabberwocks, the wailing of monsters. He could smell the sour urine odor of Death.

Don't let me come apart, don't let me break down—

And slowly, as if in response to his plea, the voices grew still and the sound of the wind faded to quiet; he had the sensation again of drifting within himself. Darkness pressed down on him—empty darkness, free of menace and terror—and he reached out for it desperately and welcomed it with the bruised planes of his mind.

Void.

133

HE AWOKE TO BIRDSONG and warm pale sunlight.

When he opened his eyes and sat up blinking, the sudden movement unleashed a wash of pain so intense in both temples it was like being struck with a blunt object. He clutched his head and leaned over with his face between his knees. Colors swam behind his eyes—blues and reds and sharp hot pulses of yellow and orange. His mouth was dry and bitter with the taste of old bile. Thoughts danced in and out of his consciousness, vague and amorphous, and he could not seem to grasp any of them.

He sat for a long while holding his head. Gradually the bright colors receded and the pain receded, and the thoughts settled into half-formed, thinly cohesive patterns. He remembered most of what had happened the night before—the barn, Tracy's capture, his escape, the blood and the candles at the fireplace—but the only memory which was vivid in every detail was the pole driven into the front lawn and what had been mounted on top of it.

His stomach convulsed, and he rolled over onto hands and knees and vomited a thin sour liquid. Kept on vomiting dryly until the effort left him weak and panting.

There was a flushed burning feel to his face as he crawled away from the odor. He thought of water, and the thought crusted the vomit residue in his mouth and made his throat close up painfully. Sitting again, he became aware of the surrounding trees, the patches of morning sunlight, a baby spruce growing out of a rotted, moss-shawled stump, a bed of delicate-looking lady ferns, a flicker knocking for grubs on a burl-swollen spruce trunk. Normal, all of it. No more of the grotesque distortion of the night.

I didn't break down, he thought.

Did I?

No. No!

When he finally gained his feet, cramped muscles made both legs as wobbly as dry sticks. He staggered once, caught onto the gray bole of a tree to keep himself from falling. Vertigo seized him: the high pine and spruce boughs, the soft blue sky above them, began to spin languidly, like a merry-go-round running at quarter speed. He squeezed his eyes shut, clinging to the tree, and kept them shut even after the dizziness passed.

Where am I? he thought.

Got to find out where I am. Let go of the tree. Walk, look for landmarks.

Jackman released the spruce bole, palms scraping over the grainy bark—and for the first time he became conscious of a sharp stinging pain in both of them and on the inside of the fingers. He shoved away and stood unsteadily with his feet planted wide apart. When he was sure he was not going to fall he turned the hands over and looked down at them and saw that they were torn and tessellated with splinters, coated with dried blood. He shuddered, put them out of sight along his sides, and took a step, another, a third: he had equilibrium again.

Walking, shuffling his feet, he looked around him. Nothing but a maze of trees and undergrowth; nothing to give him his bearings. Except the sun? Where was the sun? He stopped and craned his head back and peered up through the tops of the trees, located a small gold wedge of it. Pretty high. Must be nearly ten o'clock. He thought of his watch and glanced down at his wrist, but it was covered by black rubber. Slicker. Still wearing the oilskin. He had not realized that before either. Brain functioning like an engine on half of its cylinders, missing beats, stalling, blocking out perception. But it would repair itself—wouldn't it? He pushed back the sleeve and looked at his watch, but the crystal was broken; the hands were frozen at 11:35.

135

When he raised his head again, a filtered refraction of light made him blink. The sun. He had almost forgotten about the sun. He pivoted to face it fully. East. East was the cove, cross-island. Which direction did he want to go? *Where* did he want to go? He tried to swallow, but his throat was still closed off. Water. But the only water was at the house—

The fort. One orange left. Or was there? Yes, one orange, the juice of one orange. The fort, then: he wanted to go to the fort.

Jackman turned his body a quadrant to the left, facing north, and started walking again. Broke an irregular trail through the forest, stopping now and then to rest or when he remembered to make certain the sun remained at his right shoulder. The air grew warm, brought perspiration out of him again, but it did not occur to him to take off the slicker.

Once he thought: I don't feel as afraid as I did yesterday and last night, I don't feel the same horror. Is that because I—? Then the engine stuttered, stalled momentarily, and when it began working again the thought was gone.

He walked in a timeless state through patchworks of light and shadow. The sun climbed inexorably and thin drifting clouds veined the blue of the sky. A small brown doe appeared some distance ahead of him, came to a dead stop and keened the air and then darted away. Butterflies performed aerial acrobatics in the random beams of sunshine. There was the staccato hammering of a flicker, the singing of purple finches, the scolding chatter of chipmunks. The strong spicy scent of bayberry mingled with that of the evergreens and the faint brackish essence of the sea. But Jackman saw and heard and smelled these things without differentiation; his awareness was limited to the positioning of his body with relation to the sun and the search for familiar landmarks, for one of the island paths.

When he finally came on a landmark, he almost passed it before recognizing it for what it was. It was off on his left—a dark maze of lichen-spotted spruce and birch trunks, dead

136

lower branches jutting like gray spikes, interlocking to form a wall barring human passage. The high branches of the trees crowded together to create a canopy which the sunlight could not penetrate; the floor there was thick with damp needle humus, void of undergrowth.

Jackman halted and looked into the dense shade, and knew then that he was on the island's northwestern side, walking away from the house and the bay toward the northshore point. There was no other large section of dead and dying spruce, destroyed by dwarf mistletoe and other parasites, anywhere on the island. The fort would be at a slight angle to the east, then. The path, too, that he and Tracy had taken yesterday to the headland.

Tracy—

Keep on walking, off to the right now. Intersect the path and then go down it to the fort. And his legs moved and carried him in that direction.

THE ORANGE WAS WARM and damp and slick, and his fingers spasmed as he tried to peel it. He was sitting in the hot sun inside the fort, back rigid against the rock under the overhang, legs drawn up, elbows pressed in tight to his sides, holding the orange in both hands up close to his face. Dryness furred his tongue, lay like a thin sifting of sand across the roof of his mouth; he kept trying to swallow, anticipating the sweetness of the citrus juice, but the muscles in his throat would not dilate.

He dropped the orange twice before he managed to tear loose a piece of the skin. Then he peeled it with elaborate

137

caution, stripping away all of the white pith before he broke it into sections and lifted one to his mouth. The juice burned acidly, dissolved some of the aridness and trickled down as he tilted his head to finally penetrate the blockage in his throat. When he had sucked out the last drop of moisture, he spat the pulp to one side and repeated the process a section at a time until he had finished half the orange.

He stared at the remaining half. He wanted it badly, but the thought came that he ought to save it for later. But what would he wrap it in? The slicker was filthy, and the rest of his clothes—

What about the rest of his clothes? It occurred to him then to take the oilskin off, and he did that awkwardly and laid it across the hole scooped out of the pebbles. A sharp odor drifted up from his crotch, and when he looked down there he saw that the front of his trousers was stained and damp— one more thing he had failed to notice before. Urine. He had wet himself during the night.

That struck him funny and he burst out laughing. Some blow to the morale of the American public if they ever found out. Esteemed senator pees his pants. Wouldn't *they* be pissed off! Oh wouldn't they! Lost control of his bladder and lost control of his life and lost control of. . . .

And it was no longer funny. The laughter chopped off, and he put his chin on his chest and peered down the front of his sweater. Two buttons missing. He opened the ones that were left and took the sweater off, and the shirt underneath was wrinkled and sour with sweat and the residue of stagnant seawater. One tail hung out of his trousers like a flap of dead gray skin, and he lifted that in his free hand and examined it. Too soiled. Contaminate the orange half if he wrapped it in that. Don't have anything, then. Nothing at all.

He stared once more at the peeled half, and his mouth began to go dry again, and the sun was very hot—and he watched passively as his fingers broke it into even quarters and raised one and pushed it between his lips. He seemed able then to see inside himself, inside his mouth: blunt white teeth grinding down and shredding the segments, sweet juice flowing backward and down the long dark blistered cavern into the hollow below. Fascinating. Worth watching a second time. And his fingers and teeth responded, and the juice ran, soothed, and then there was nothing left but pulp and pith. Pulp and pith and piss, he thought. Piss and pith and pulp. So much for the problem of the orange.

Now what?

Did it matter? They'd find him sooner or later, and when they did they would cut off his head like they cut off Tracy's. Or something worse. Was there something worse?

One, two! One, two! And through and through the vorpal blade went snicker-snack!

Oh yes, not much doubt about it now: the island and the game belonged to the Jabberwocks. . . .

The sun's heat was making him drowsy, a little sick. Too hot here in the open. Sunstroke. Bake his brain like bread dough in an oven. Shouldn't be sitting here at all. Should get up and go—

Where?

Round and round, round and round.

Sleep, he thought. Sleep?

He examined that prospect with critical detachment. Good, a good stratagem. Sleep was a panacea for most ills, anybody could tell you that. When you didn't feel right in mind and body, you slept. Healing sleep.

But not here. Some place dark and cool, hidden, where they couldn't find him with their vorpal blade. The woods? Not secure enough, not dark enough.

The caves.

Of course—the caves.

He looked up at the coppery glare of the sun. One o'clock, maybe one-thirty. The tide would start to ebb around three; he could get down into the biggest of the caves then, and he could stay in there until well after midnight. Cool, damp, dark, safe.

Standing, he stared over the top of one boulder. Nothing

in the trees but trees. He started out through the seaward opening, and then stopped. The slicker. Take the slicker along, going to need it tonight for the cold. Sweater too. And the tin of Spam and the last chocolate bar; have to eat eventually.

When he put the food into one of the oilskin's pockets, he discovered that it had been empty. The other one too. He could not remember having lost the flashlight and the knife, but he no longer had them. No longer had the binoculars either, for Christ's sake. Gone, all gone.

He rolled the sweater into a cylindrical shape and stuffed it inside one of the sleeves and folded the oils over his right arm. Stepped out onto the point, came around along the cobbles, and went up again into the forest.

THERE WAS A STRONG northeast wind blowing across the cliff flat, making fluttery sounds among the blueberry shrubs, creating a humming counterpoint to the hiss of the rote. The sun was westering now, hazed by pale cloud drifts: close to four o'clock. It had taken him nearly three hours to come less than two miles, and he had had to pull himself from tree to tree on the last long rise; but he had not fallen a single time. Pyrrhic victory, and not much of a one at that. Just a single completed move on the gameboard. Win a battle, lose the war. Mix the mixed-up metaphors.

Sleep, he thought, got to sleep.

He moved to the edge of the woods, cast furtive looks in both directions along the flat. Deserted. On his left he had a glimpse of the stone altar, wrenched his head away. He stumbled out onto the flat, the slicker trailing from his right hand, then checked himself and forced his weakening legs to carry him heel-and-toe toward the edge of the cliff.

The way down to the caves was well over to the west, through a long narrow cut spotted with blue-green algae. When he got to there and stood on the edge and looked down to where waves lifted thin sheets of spray over a jumble of rocks exposed by the tide, vertigo overcame him again, and he had to sit down hard on his buttocks to keep himself from tumbling over. The dizziness vanished almost immediately, but instead of getting up again he used his hands to push his body forward until his legs were dangling down inside the cut.

Long way to the bottom, much longer than he remembered it; but it had been twenty years since his last visit to the caves, and he had been young and agile then. Have to use both hands: put the slicker on, button it up. He took the rolled-up sweater out of the sleeve, got into that first and then donned the oilskin.

When he was ready he eased himself down, back braced into the hollow, fingers clutching at crevices in the rough rock walls. Directly below was a wide flat-topped shelf covered with rubbery brown rockweed, and just above it the cut showed the black-brown presence of barnacles. He lifted his hands at that point and got his feet planted on the shelf and lowered to palms and knees. A small green crab scuttled out in front of him, pivoted and snapped its claws menacingly. Jackman stared at it, not moving: mute confrontation. The crab retreated finally, went down along the side of the shelf and out of sight.

He crawled ten feet and then turned his body, hanging onto the slippery seaweed, and swung his legs over and found purchase on a narrow jutting ledge. Across the ledge and a short step downward were a staggered row of three rounded outcroppings diminishing in height by four feet each, like a crude staircase. Rockweed and sea lettuce matted

141

the rocks and made the footing treacherous; but he got down them with no difficulty, no damage except a fresh cut in one palm from the shell of a mussel.

One last stratified shelf shawled in red-brown Irish moss, a tide pool in a pocket on its outer lip teeming with sea urchins and anemones. Spray stung his face, clung glistening in tiny beads to the oilskin as he dropped onto the shelf, stepped off it onto a slender strip that fronted the first and highest of the caves.

There were three of them, the other two set side by side in a deep cleft twenty-five feet farther down, where laminarias swayed in the pounding wash of surf between the jumble of exposed rocks at the cliff base. Those two were shallow, with mouths so low you had to enter them on all fours. This one was much larger, extending some fifty feet into the cliff wall, wide enough near its deepest perimeter for a man to stand stooped over or to lie stretched out full length.

A milky translucent moon jellyfish flowed over the rock at the opening to the cave like a sentry barring admittance. Jackman kicked at it, sent it sliding away, and then hunched his shoulders and bent at the waist and went inside. A crab scurried past his foot; an anemone attached to the base of the wall waved faintly luminescent tentacles. Fifteen feet in, the rock was coated with coarse sand and cobbles and deposits of kelp and flotsam, and the light became murky and there was the thick dank raw-salt odor peculiar to seawater caves. Cool in there, too—almost cold: he had forgotten just how chill it could be. And it would get colder still after the sun went down.

Too late to worry about that now. The hell with that.

Sleep.

After forty feet there was no light at all except for the pale sphere of the cave mouth. Jackman stopped there and swung his foot loosely over the floor. More kelp, more chunks of shale and granite; he scraped out a cleared space, a bed for himself. Jonas had taught him that there was nothing to fear in these caves except perhaps the green crabs, but they

142

would not bother you if you were motionless; the sting of the moon jellies was not poisonous, not even a mild irritant.

Fatigue drove him to his knees. His arm felt heavy as he raised it to pull the slicker's hood over his head. He let himself collapse onto his side, got a forearm under his chin; his eyes closed and instantly warm darkness seeped in to blanket his mind. The last things he heard were the constant thrashing of the surf, the hollow whispering of the wind, the faint dripping of water from the ceiling and on the walls, on the walls. . . .

I dreamt I dwelt in marble halls, and each damp thing that creeps and crawls went wobble-wobble on the walls. . . .

The Jabberwock stood ten feet tall and had flaming red eyes and a scaly corpus on which a black-magic symbol had been painted; its hands bore long gleaming yellow claws, and one of them clenched a sword with the head of an ax at the tip, bright-stained and dripping. It loomed over him, swinging the vorpal blade in a malevolent arc, its manxome mouth open and fangs like saffron-colored daggers spotted with bits of gristled meat forming an obscene leer.

"Your head," the Jabberwock said, "for the blood of the frumious Bandersnatch."

And he began to laugh. Even though his body cringed away, eyes fixed on the seesawing blade, he could not control himself and the laughter spilled out of his throat and rang madly in the stillness. The Jabberwock swung the vorpal blade up, swung it down—snicker-snack!—and Jackman's head rolled across the stone floor, still laughing wildly, and bounced against the wall and came to rest aslant.

"Wobble-wobble," he said. "Wobble-wobble."

The blade made clanking sounds, like chains dragging, as the Jabberwock lowered it heavily at its feet and began to back away. Growling sounds, burbling sounds, came from its open mouth.

Jackman watched his body get up and come forward and

143

reach down and pick up his head, fit it carefully on the severed stem of his neck.

The Jabberwock darted behind a pillar, hiding.

"Come out, come out, wherever you are," he said, and ran to the pillar—but the creature was gone, there was nothing there except a puddle of fresh blood. He knelt and touched the blood with his fingers, and it turned to water, turned to dust, and the wind came and blew the dust away.

He started walking, looking for the Jabberwock. It was there; where was it? Come out, come out!

Something came out, but it was not the Jabberwock. It was Meg, and she was wearing a lavender evening gown.

Frowning, he said, "What are you doing here?"

"What are *you* doing here?" Meg said, and laughed shrilly.

"Stop it, stop that."

"You're such a fool, David. You've always been such a fool."

"Is that so?"

"Yes. I won't be sorry when you're dead."

"Do you hate me that much?"

"I don't hate you. I don't feel anything for you."

"You don't feel anything, period."

"I suppose you think you do."

"Yes. I loved you once, I tried to make it work—"

"That's all you've ever done, *try* to make things work," she said. "Try to make our marriage work, try to make your political career work, try to make your life work. The only thing you ever really *made* work was that film of yours in college. If you had chosen filmmaking over politics, you'd have been a doer instead of a tryer, David."

"I tried to stand up to the Old Man—"

"Tried. There, you see what I mean?"

"Damn it, *you* wanted me to go into politics as much as he did. If I had had your support. . . ."

". . . you would have done just exactly what you did do," Meg said. "You couldn't stand up to me any more than you

144

could to him. You fool, we manipulated you and you let it happen. People have been manipulating you all your life. You're like the camera in *I, Camera, Eye*—useless by yourself; you need someone to activate you, focus you, so you can open your shutter-eyes and see and record. . . ."

"I don't want to hear any more of this," he said. "I have to find the Jabberwock."

The sound of her laughter echoed hollowly as he walked away.

He turned a corner, and sitting on one of the walls was the Old Man. Dressed in a black business suit with a narrow-striped tie, but on top of his head was perched a red, white and blue Uncle Sam hat. The forefinger of his right hand probed gently, exploratorily, at one nostril, and he held a curved clay pipe in a corner of his mouth.

"Survival is a game, just like everything else," the Old Man said. "If you want to survive, you've got to keep thinking of it that way. Start planning strategy: move and countermove."

"The Jabberwock cut off my head," Jackman said, "and I put it back on. But I can't do that with Tracy's head. She's dead for all time."

"What's done is done. What does it matter if you lose a pawn as long as the king remains untouched."

"You son of a bitch, she was a human being!"

"Pawn," the Old Man said obstinately. "They're all pawns, just pieces on the board."

"But I'm not, is that it?"

"You are if you want to be."

"Meaning what?"

"Meaning that it's all up to you."

"But this isn't even a *game* anymore—"

"Of course it is," the Old Man said, and raised a hand. "Everything is a game, and this above all—" There was a clicking in his voice, like that of a switch being thrown, and he broke off. Then: "Of course it is," he said, and raised a hand. "Everything is a game, and this above all—" Click. "Of course it

145

is," he said, and raised a hand. "Everything is a game, and this above all—" Click. "Of course it is. . . ."

Jackman hurried down a long corridor. There was somebody standing at the far end, in front of a dark archway, and when he approached he saw that it was his brother Dale.

"Hello, Dale," he said. "Have you seen the Jabberwock?"

Dale did not answer him; instead he walked over by one of the walls. Jackman could see into the dark archway by then, and there were a lot of people in there. They began to file out one by one: Charlie Pepper. Richard Nixon. Alan Pennix. Senator Lawton. Linda Fong. His mother. A crippled Vietnam veteran. Jonas. Miss Bigelow. James Turner. Fred Tremaine. Gerald Ford. Alicia. A May Day demonstrator. Walter Cronkite. Judy Tremaine. J. Edgar Hoover. The three-piece band from Milbridge. Lyndon Johnson. A dozen more. None of these said anything to him or looked at him either.

All of them formed a tight circle, arms around each other's shoulders, and put their heads together, whispering—and the Jabberwock jumped out of a dark niche and whirled the vorpal sword in a long sweeping arc and cut off all their heads, sent their heads rolling and rattling like marbles on the damp marble walls. Then, burbling, the creature capered away again and the clanking of the ax blade diminished into silence.

Jackman went over to the collapsed and headless bodies, peered down at them. And one sprang up, startling him because it was not headless after all; the Jabberwock had missed one, and the one it had missed was the only black one, Charlie Pepper.

"I'm glad it didn't get you, Charlie," he said.

"Ain't no Jabberwock goin to hurt a smart old nigger like me," Charlie Pepper said. "Don't seem like it hurt you neither, boy—at least not bad as it could've."

He giggled. "Cut off my head, but I put it back on."

"You got it back on straight?"

"I don't know," he said. "Is it straight?"

146

"Close, maybe; then again, maybe not. You goin to have to get it fastened down tight. Elsewise, your eyes goin to see crooked and you goin to stumble, and then it'll fall right off again. Maybe for good."

"All right. Charlie, you think I can find the Jabberwock and take the vorpal blade away and lop off *its* head?"

But Charlie Pepper had vanished.

He sat down on one of the walls, and a damp thing wobbled there, and he was suddenly very cold. His neck throbbed where the sword had sliced through it. He raised his hands to his head, probed it with his fingers. Was it on straight?

Pretty close, anyway.

Pretty close.

HE WAS SITTING UP against the jagged wall of the cave, shivering, staring into the darkness. Surf ran hissingly, close to the entrance, and the wind whistled and carried droplets of spray like a fine mist; the rote had a restless booming cadence. Faint furry gray at the cave mouth. Night. And cold—damp, numbing. The skin on his exposed face and hands felt brittle, as if it had been frozen over with thin crusts of ice.

He did not remember waking or lifting his body into the seated position; he was simply awake and sitting there. His temples ached, and dryness had closed his throat again, and there was a crick in his neck caused by his sleeping posture, and sharp pain fluctuated under his breastbone in a bodily protest against hunger. He imagined he could hear his cold-stiffened joints creaking audibly every time he moved.

Thoughts seemed far away, dulled. Not many details on

the morning, the afternoon, the fort, the trek here to the cliffs, the climb downward over the rocks; all like things you had done a long, long time ago, only dimly recalled and with uncertain accuracy. Once, at the age of twelve, he had had an appendectomy, and when he had come out of the anaesthesia his mind had felt like this: drugged, muted, aware but not quite aware. Not unpleasant, but not pleasant either. Things drifting around and around that you wanted to catch hold of—speculations, memories, stratagems—but they darted away like tadpoles in a murky pool when you reached out for them.

Concentrate. Food. Tin of Spam, chocolate bar: he slid his hand into the slicker pocket to make sure they were still there. But he knew as he did so that he would not be able to force anything down his constricted throat. Should not have eaten the whole orange this afternoon. If he could not get fresh water—and it seemed certain he could not—what else was there that contained liquid? Berries? Were there any blueberries or strawberries on those shrubs and patches on the flat? Yes, but they would be green now, inedible. Didn't ripen until late June. Anything else? Nothing else.

Feeling. What did he feel? Cold. Pain. Fear? Grief or guilt for Tracy and what had happened to her? Any emotion? Only the numbness of his body; at this moment, only that.

Time. Late now. The tide was starting to come in, he could judge that by the sound of the surf, the windblown moisture. After midnight, maybe. Better get out of here, get out of the damp cold, climb up the rocks before the breakers came in heavy enough to slick them dangerously. First matter of attention, this. First things first, first moves first.

And he gained his feet, leaning on the wall, and stood for a moment working kinks out of his arms and legs; then he made his way laboriously along the moist rock, through the deposits of kelp, and out through the cave mouth. Foam slithered against the side of the flattish shelf to his left, which meant the other two caves were submerged now; one of the breakers splashed up high and drenched him. The sea was dark, mist-free, choppy—short steep whitecaps riding the tops of long swells. No moon tonight? He looked up, and there were thick black-rimmed clouds scudding rapidly to the west. The pull of the wind out here was strong, cutting, and the air was permeated with the metallic smell of ozone. Gulls wheeled in nervous dogfight patterns.

Summer squall building, he thought.

Then he thought: Squall—rain. Rain.

He *could* get fresh water after all.

But first he had to get up to the flat, and quickly; he couldn't be climbing on these rocks when it broke. How much longer? Not long, clouds massing at a good clip. Half an hour, maybe less.

He tipped his head back and stared up the cliff face, and it looked impossibly high, it looked as if it extended far enough into the sky to touch the running clouds. Don't think about that; you've scaled it dozens of times before, you got down here tonight and you can get back up again. Find a handhold on the near shelf—and he did that and pulled his body atop it. Like pulling up the dead blackfish he and Jonas had discovered floating in the sea one morning when they went out to run the lobster traps, all bloated and stone-heavy.

Spray licked at the nape of his neck where the slicker's hood had fallen back. He half-turned to press thighs and stomach against the first of the stepping stones, feet planting solidly, fingers groping for new purchase. Heave up! And he was on the outcropping and reaching out for the second one. Firm grip with both hands. Heave up! Third outcropping. Heave up!

He knelt there for a moment, rasping in his lungs like a file on wood. Don't look down, don't look up. The ledge next, watch out for those loose bunches of seaweed, watch out for barnacles and mussels. He hooked into a crevice on the ledge, lifted, but his foot slipped and for a dizzying moment he seemed to hang there, legs flailing, his other hand grabbing desperately for a second handhold. Got it—got the toe of his shoe wedged into another fissure in the rock and steadied himself and then hoisted prone on the ledge and lay still until the strain in his arms lessened.

Worst part of the climb coming up. Slippery rockweed on that wide flat shelf; the long cut that you had to go up the same way you came down, facing away, back braced and making inching progress with hips and heels and hands. Used to do it with no trouble at all except once in a while a cut or a scrape. And what happened to the boy I was then? Where did he go, when did I lose him?

Stand up—slow, lean against the cliff wall. Fingers scuttling like crabs over the rockweed, nails scraping, chipping; tug, and puffy ropes of it came free. He flung them away, found a rocky projection that he could curl his hand around, tested it. Solid. Other hand now, and a water-filled cup deep enough and wide enough to allow a palmhold with fingers splayed. Elbows locked, muscles taut, knees struggling for leverage . . . just a little more, pull! . . . and his body wiggled onto the shelf and slid across the slick weed matting to the center.

Rest a moment again. Then a slow bellyslide to the bottom of the cut: sea wracks like a waxed floor under his body, little effort necessary. Careful now, careful. Over onto his right hip, onto his buttocks, arms lifting back above his head, hands probing for the bare rock beyond the line where the barnacles had welded themselves rough and sharp-edged. Anchored hold, legs tenting, heels digging in. Now hoist up again; unfold at the waist. Shooting pains in both forearms—and one heel skidded loose, went out at an angle; but the other one held fast and he arched back hard into the cut and wedged there while he got the one leg pulled in and then jacked down into the base pocket.

Sixty feet below, the angry surf hammered against the rocks.

He kept his eyes straight ahead, looking out toward the

150

nesting islets offshore, as he brought his hands down to arm-pit level and located other crannies and knobs. Thighs spread slightly, knees flexed, and—squirm, twist, pull, shove up. Two feet, maybe. Rest. Different holds, make sure they're firm. Again. Two more feet. Rest. Different holds. Again—

Slipped, body slipping and scraping downward.

He jammed his wrists, jammed his thighs and shoulders against the rock. Heard the oilskin rip on a barnacle or horny projection. Momentum ceased, but he had lost three or four feet. Agony in his palms, feeling of suffocation. But only fifteen feet left, and the last six or seven of that more easily accessible because the cut bellied deeper into the cliff wall, and you could turn around at that point and pretty much crawl out. Almost there. Almost there.

Holds, shove and pull, rest. Holds, shove and pull, rest. Holds, shove and pull, rest. And his hips and sides felt the inward turn of the rock, and he gave one last push, and he was sitting tilted forward in the depression. Rest. Then one leg pulling up and in, bracing, and buttocks gyrating upward; he turned on his side, looked up, and he could see the edge of the flat and the black tops of trees in the distance, the roiling swarm of clouds obliterating the night sky. And then he dragged himself up the rest of the way on his side in one hauling, scrabbling movement, threw his body out of the cut and lay spread-eagled, breath wheezing through his nostrils, on the wet grass of the flat.

The staggered, drumming beat of his heart was so loud that he was unable to hear the rote or the wind. He did not move, waiting for the feeling of suffocation to abate, for his muscles to unknot. The wind stung his cheeks, wailing emptily across the open space, and under its driving force the sea purled in a turbulent rhythm; the smell of ozone was sharper. The squall would hit the island any minute now.

And he shouldn't be out here either when it did, exposed; if the blow got strong enough, it could pitch a man right off the edge. Into the trees, he thought. Catch as much of the rainwater in his hands as he could and drink his fill and then wait out the squall in some kind of shelter: one of the rock formations, a burrow under a deadfall. After that—

After that was after that.

Heart gentling, constriction easing in his throat. Get up now. And he drew himself into a hump at the middle, got his head and shoulders up until he was kneeling, and then made it to his feet. Swayed. Lifted one hand to his eyes to rub away salty wetness. Blinked and looked over toward the woods.

And one of them was standing there.

Just standing there beside a blueberry bush, naked to the waist, cradling a rifle against the dark symbol on the bare skin of his chest.

Jackman's mouth hinged open and he stared in dumb fascination, heard himself make a moaning sound. Reality shimmered, dissolved dreamily. He took a faltering step to his right, a second, then swung his body and started to run— and ran six steps before he saw the second one coming toward him at an angle from where the stone altar stood, carrying something long and flat.

Ax!

No, he said, oh God no!

But it wasn't an ax, it was a board. . . .

He looked back frantically, and the first one had started to advance, they were converging on him and he had nowhere to run, the cliff was at his flank and he did not have enough time to go back down through the cut. I'm dreaming this too, he thought, but knew that he was not, not this time, and he tried to run straight ahead, and they drifted over to cut him off. He changed direction in midstride, panic raking at him, and ran shambling at the second one; nerve-endings screamed, it felt as though he were moving at a retarded speed. Then everything seemed to slow down, to happen with incredible precision: his arms opened out and his head lowered and he reached out for the one with the board, but that one stepped aside agilely and Jackman stumbled and

152

lost his balance and started to fall, and it took a long, long time for him to strike the ground, jarring on his knees, on his elbows, and then to roll over gagging and stare up with bulging eyes—and the Jabberwock was looming over him, vorpal board held high over its right shoulder. He cried out, saw the board come forward and down in a graceful slanting arc toward the side of his head, and thought to bring an arm up to protect himself, and began to raise the arm against the manxome thrust—

Snicker-snack!

Too late.

PART FOUR

Monday, May 25: THE ISLAND

With tight-strung bow a wick'd hunter I became—
Its quivering tension
Bespeaks the hunter's powerful dimension—
Beware and flee: this arrow's dangerous aim
Is like none other: this is not a game!

—Nietzsche, "Postlude" to *Beyond Good and Evil*

PITCH BLACKNESS, the faint hollow drumming of rain.

Odor of fermented apples.

Thudding pain along the left side of his head.

Thirst.

Cold hard surface under him; cramps in both legs, a tingling sensation in his right arm. He groaned, moved over onto his stomach, and the tingling increased: he had been lying on the arm. He lifted a shaky hand and touched the pain. Pulpy, but there was not any blood that he could feel.

First thought: Still got my head—didn't cut off my head after all.

He pushed up slowly to all fours. Giddiness, nausea. Fever chills capered between his shoulder blades, and his face felt hot and swollen again, caked with salt freeze. Damp all over, clothes sticking clammily to his skin. In a detached way he wondered if he could be coming down with pneumonia.

Pulling back on his knees, he rested the weight of his buttocks against his upthrust heels. Loose tension to his muscles, like ropes too often knotted and stretched. Breathing shallow and irregular. Sea-pulse in both temples now, as well as

157

in the pulpy region over his left ear. Torn and splintered palms stinging, throbbing, where they rested flat against his thighs.

Any strength left? Enough—always seemed to be just enough. He extended both arms, groped through the darkness. Fingertips touched a rough vertical surface at an angle to his right. Leaning that way, he ran his knuckles along it. Wall. Fieldstone wall. He crawled closer, got a shoulder pressed to it, and used it as a fulcrum to hoist himself weakly erect.

Lying, kneeling, standing—up and down continually for the past . . . what? Thirty-six hours? In and out of consciousness, in and out of pain. But this time his nerves were almost quiet and his mind seemed to be remarkably uncluttered, lucid, as if the blow delivered on the cliffs had driven all the hazy confusion straight out of his head.

And he realized he was afraid again.

He concentrated on the fear, and it was not nearly as stark or crippling as before and during his entrapment in the barn, immediately after his discovery of Tracy's severed head. Just an undercurrent, rippling: watery reflections of death and horror. But rippling there too were rage and hatred and something else too murky to perceive. Feeling—he had regained the capacity to *feel*.

Irrelevant right now. Survival was the only thing that mattered.

The apple smell was overpowering.

Apples, he thought—and knew abruptly where he was. The only place on the island where apples were stored was the fruit cellar under Jonas' cottage. Jonas had a small pot still set up there in which he manufactured a few gallons of applejack each year for his own private use. Claimed he made the best applejack in the state of Maine. Down East white lightning, the Old Man always said, and everyone would laugh.

Why had they put him here?

Why was he still alive?

158

Because they're in no hurry, he thought; because they feed on terror as much as on blood. They want me conscious when the time comes, like Tracy must have been.

But the explanation did not satisfy him. Something wrong with it. More to it than that—or less to it than that. They—

He could not pursue it, not yet.

Survival. Escape.

Visualize the cellar. Narrow, fairly long. Stairs leading down from the kitchen in the middle of the inner wall. Shelving on the left, crates of apples. Wood-and-copper cooker and mash box and fermentation barrel on that side, in the juncture with the outer wall; water heater there too, and an oil furnace, and a maze of copper and steel and galvanized tin piping. Firewood stacked against the outer wall, and high above, where the wood siding of the cottage joined the field-stone foundation, a large window hinged so that you could swing it inward. He seemed to remember a small standing freezer along the right-hand wall, but nothing else that might be there.

The door. Sure to be locked. Unless one of them was sitting up there in the kitchen, waiting for him to try coming out, waiting to take him someplace then where the candles would burn on a pagan altar—

No.

The window. Storm shutters riveted to the outside wall: would they have thought to close and lock them? Easy for him to get out if they hadn't—too easy. And those shutters were made of heavy wood reinforced with iron bands, fitted with iron lockbolts that snapped into rings top and bottom; forty years of gale-force winds had been unable to break them open once they were locked down.

There was no other way out of the cellar.

The undercurrent of fear grew stronger; his genitals tightened into a ligature. Stay calm, don't lose control again. Check out the window and the door: find out for certain the way things stand.

Orientation. Which part of the cellar was he in? Bare stone

159

wall here. He extended his arms again and shuffle-stepped to his left. Three paces, four—and he came up against something hard at waist level, bumping it with his hip; above it, his hands still slid over empty stone. He turned into the object, reached down to touch it, found its top smooth and flat and cold. The standing freezer. Right-hand wall, then; stairs diagonally to his left, outer wall to his right.

He hesitated. Light in the freezer?

His fingers found the edge of the lid, pulled it up. A rush of icy air, but no light. He lowered the lid again.

There were half a dozen large-wattage bulbs in sockets on the ceiling joists, a switch on the wall beside the door. But getting there would take time, and he didn't need light to examine the window or find a weapon. Those things first and foremost.

He reversed direction, and when he came to the corner he turned his body to face the rear wall and eased along there, arms raised and hands exploring the wood siding just above the level of his forehead. After half a dozen paces his fingers touched the frame of the window. When he found the catch at the bottom, he flipped it loose and pulled back slowly, and the window hinged inward with a faint creaking sound. He drew it open as far as it would go, and the voice of the squall increased in volume—but he felt none of the wind, none of the rain.

Even before his fingers bent against unresisting wood and iron banding, he knew the storm shutters had been secured outside.

He put his back to the wall, teeth clenched, and moved further to his right. Almost immediately his hand touched a solid but yielding object—pine log—and felt it loosen and begin to slide away before he could catch hold of it. It tumbled down, thumping, like something rolling down a short flight of stairs, and then banged into the cement floor and was still. After-echoes faded through the blackness. He held his breath, listening.

160

No sounds from inside the cottage; no sounds at all except the steady, distant rhythm of wind slapping and hurling rain at the clapboards, at the pitched sides of the roof.

He lowered both hands, carefully, and probed the stack of firewood. Got a firm grip on another of the cut logs and brought it in against his chest. Three feet long, maybe eight inches in diameter. Good.

Now—the door.

The staircase would be fifty feet or so directly in front of him, he judged, and the floor across to it should be clear. He could go around to the stairs by way of the walls, use them to brace his body; but if he could not walk without support, now was the time to find it out. Step away from the fieldstones. Legs jellied, not much feeling in either foot. Shuffle forward in a straight line, heel and toe, sodden shoes making thin liquid noises; both arms stretched out in front of him, hands and the piece of firewood transcribing small, tentative arcs. Must be almost there now—

One toe stubbed against something, then the ankle, and his legs gave way at once, and he sprawled out sideways over the obstacle, came down hard on it and on a second one like it. Slender strips of wood dug into his thigh, his upper right arm; the firewood skidded away. The heel of his hand dislodged several small round things, sent them bouncing and rolling away. Apples. Apple crates. He dragged himself off to one side and crouched on the floor, head raised, listening again.

The cottage above remained silent.

He did not try to stand again: too much pain, old and new, sharp and dull. Instead he crawled around the crates, brushing away spilled apples, hunting for the cordwood. Found it, clutched it. Kept on crawling until he came up against the bottom runner of the staircase.

He looked up to where the door was, but the heavy black let him see nothing at all. No strip of light beneath the door, then, but that did not have to mean anything. One of them

161

could still be up there in the kitchen, sitting in the dark, patient. Creatures of the darkness, like vampires, like Jabberwocks. . . .

Up the stairs on his knees, a runner at a time, hanging onto the railing. He made small bumping sounds that he could not avoid, but clamped lips and teeth to muffle the audible rasp of his breath. When he reached the narrow landing he sat there on one hip and put his ear to the panel. Unbroken stillness. He laid the pine log across his right shoulder, cocking it, and got his left hand up and wrapped around the doorknob. Turned it counterclockwise, half a rotation. The latch did not click, did not release; the knob bound against its lock.

Jackman tugged once, gently, to see whether or not the door was fitted tightly into the jamb, and when it did not yield he released the knob and let his hand fall bonelessly into his lap.

Break it down? Not much chance: the panels were thick, the latch securely fastened. Noise factor, too; he did not know if one of them was close enough to hear some or all of whatever he did in here. Pick the lock? He had no knowledge of how to pick locks, and no tools besides.

Scratch off the door along with the window. Scratch off the only two exits from the cellar.

Escapeproof locked room. . . .

TIME.

Seconds running, sliding away.

It might be hours before they decided to come for him, and it might only be minutes. He could not waste any more

162

time sitting here frustrated; all he was doing was waiting for death. Think. Work out a plan. Keep himself together.

Options. He could stay up here on the landing or hide under the stairs and try to overpower them with the firewood when they showed themselves. But the landing was too small for maneuverability, and the door opened into the kitchen, and he was too weak and battered to be effective in a fight, and they were far too cunning not to anticipate some kind of attack and take precautions against it. Was there anything he had forgotten about or that Jonas had added since the last time he had been in here? Anything he could use as a more powerful weapon, as a possible means of escape?

He struggled onto his feet, using the railing and the firewood for leverage. Fumbled along the wall, felt out the plastic casing of the light switch. Flipped the toggle up.

Nothing happened.

Up and down again, and a third time. Empty clicks. Bastards had taken out the bulbs, or thrown the main on the fusebox, or cut the goddamn wiring. He turned away and leaned on the railing and stared down into the heavy darkness.

Matches, he thought.

Firewood for the cooker, you had to have matches to touch it off. And he seemed to recall that Jonas kept candles down here in case of generator failure. There had to be matches, then; Jonas didn't smoke, he had no particular reason to carry matches or a lighter on his person. The shelving. They ought to be on the shelving near the still.

He went down the stairs, supporting most of his weight on the railing. When he reached the floor he dropped onto his knees again because he did not want to risk another fall, pushed forward among the scattered apples to the first of the crates. They were set three abreast, and he moved laterally along them to his left, toward the shelving and the wall. Beyond the last crate in the row was a narrow space large enough for him to pass into: aisleway that Jonas had left clear so he could get to the shelves. Jackman reached out and

163

his fingers contacted a vertical board, then filled mason canning jars on one of the shelves.

He became sharply aware of the arid burning in his mouth and throat, the cracked surfaces of his lips. Liquid—Jonas' applejack? Better not: that stuff was like bottled fire, and in his condition, on a tender empty stomach, even a little would do more damage than good. He had to keep his thoughts clear if he was going to have any chance at all.

Straightening up, he probed higher. More jars, nothing but jars here. The next tier, knee-walking. Larger jars and quart bottles, some empty, some full. Another tier. Lower shelves vacant, dusty. Upper ones: galvanized tin fittings, asbestos sheeting, pieces of copper tubing, a dented pail, a tray of sheet metal nails, a small tackhammer. He weighed the tackhammer for a moment, put it back. Too small, too light to be of any use as a weapon.

Jackman crawled further and his hand brushed over a coiled length of something thick and rubbery on the floor. Hose. He started to push it aside, stopped with his hand on it. Water. Christ, you needed water to run a still too; there was a faucet down here. But where? The hose was not attached to it—just lying there in a coil. Can't remember, but it had to be close by, close to the still.

Matches.

Primary objective was matches. With light he could find the faucet quickly; with light he could stand up, move around, search the cellar. Forget about water for now.

He shoved at the hose, felt it slide less than six inches and then bunch up against a solid obstruction. A leaning, fingertip examination told him it was a network of piping, and beyond it, the cool metal side of the oil furnace. Near the corner now; the tier of shelves on his left would be the last one. No matches here, then there weren't any matches at all.

Bottom shelf. Empty. Next one. Empty. Next one. Six-ounce cans of something, a small wood-handled tool with a flat squarish blade. Putty knife. Not very sharp, not very useful, but he caught it up anyway, on impulse, and put it into the pocket of his slicker. Next shelf, stretched up on his knees. Empty.

He would have to stand to get to the ones at the top. He hooked his fingers onto one of the horizontal boards and tugged down, testing the tier's sturdiness. Wobbly. If he tried to use it as a fulcrum, he might bring the whole thing crashing down on top of him. He fumbled over the piping, got his hand through it and onto the top edge of the furnace, and used that to bring himself upright.

When he had his balance he turned back to the shelves and swept a palm gently across the one at chest height. Five-pound sack of sugar. A funnel. An earthenware jug. An open box filled with smooth, waxy cylinders—candles. But there was nothing else on the shelf.

Next one above, fingers searching with desperation now. Empty, only dust—

And then his hand closed over something in the left-hand corner, felt the rough sandpaper strip along both sides. Matchbox, kitchen matches. He grabbed it, almost blundered it away in his haste, hung on and dragged it down and held it to his chest. Rattling inside: nearly full. He slid it open and took out one of the sticks, reclosed it. Had to will his hands steady as he pressed the tip against the rough strip, scraped it, scraped it a second time.

Light flared, half-blinded him, and then settled into a wavering flame. Blinking, he held the match out in front of him, saw the labyrinth of piping and copper coils, the boxy shape of the furnace, the water heater behind it and the still arrangement a few feet away to the right. Apple crates behind him, floor unoccupied at the front of the cooker and across to where the firewood was stacked.

The matchlight flickered, began to die hotly against his thumb. He shook it out, dropped it, got another one from the box and struck that. This time he used the light to locate the candles, take one out. When he had the wick burning steadily, he put the matchbox into his slicker pocket and stepped toward the pot boiler, around it. The candle flame cast a weird, fluttery glow on the darkness, created mobile shadows—and let him see the faucet jutting out of the field-stone wall adjacent to the water heater.

Jackman went to the faucet, sank down beside it. The burning thirst in his mouth and throat was so intense that he could not move his tongue. Turn the T-handle slowly, don't want more than a trickle, don't want any more noise; hold the candle out of the way. There—and the valve released and the water came spilling out.

He twisted and ducked his head under the tap, let the icy liquid splash over his face, pour into his mouth. The first cascade seemed to back up against the blockage in his throat; then the muscles relaxed, and he was able to swallow, gagging, gasping audibly in spite of himself. Spasmodic gulps until the dryness was gone, until his stomach convulsed. Enough: you could drink yourself sick when you were this dehydrated. He forced his mouth shut, turned the handle to stop the flow.

The water energized him, gave him a fresh surge of strength; he was able to get up again without aid. He held the candle down low enough so that he could see the floor, oblivious to the hot dripping of wax, and went to his left, hunched over. Quarter cord of the firewood, a small pile of kindling; but no hatchet or other wood-splitting tool. Bare wall under the window and around to where the freezer stood—the right-angled area he had covered blindly earlier.

He crossed beyond the freezer. In the upper cellar corner and along the wall beneath the stairs were drums of oil for the furnace, more five-pound sacks of sugar, two large bags of potatoes. He came back to the foot of the stairs and went around the apple crates to the shelving. Down the aisleway, looking now in the shimmery candlelight at the stored things he had identified by feel. Random objects that he'd missed in the darkness, but nothing usable in any way.

Full circuit, search completed; nothing overlooked. And he was still trapped, still helpless. No way out. Sacrificial sheep penned up and awaiting slaughter.

166

Standing in the shadows by the pot still, he ran splayed fingers over his face. No choice now except to try battering at the door and keep on battering at it until it opened or, much more probably, they came for him. Impotent rage and hatred became as strong as the fear; he was not going to give up, they would have to knock him out again or drag him off kicking and fighting.

He started to turn, bringing the candle around, and then stopped abruptly. He was facing in toward the corner, and something had caught his attention, started an urgent tickling at the back of his mind. Arm at full extension, he rocked the candle flame from side to side. Focus on the half-born perception. The furnace? Simple oil-burner, frame made of galvanized sheet metal. Gravity feed—

And he had it: not the furnace, the thick round length of cold-air duct pipe that extended up from its top into a box flashing between two of the ceiling joists.

His heart beat faster, skipping tempo. He stepped around the still, moved in as close to the furnace as he could get. The pipe had to be twenty inches in diameter, and that meant the opening covered by the flashing overhead was the same. Big enough for a man his size to fit through; no obstructions in the duct box set through the floor—just a floor register in the room directly above, and you could push that out of the way with one hand.

Christ, sweet Christ, if he could dismantle that pipe. . . .

Hope and urgency mingled inside him, providing stimulus. He shoved lightly against the duct. Sturdy, but it had a snap joint in the middle, no caulking compound or nails. Have to get up on top of the furnace in order to break it loose. Then pry the flashing free, nothing but sheet-metal nails holding it to the ceiling.

He paused to listen. The rain seemed to be slackening now, and you could no longer hear the wind slapping at the sides and eaves of the cottage. Except for an occasional creaking, nothing stirred anywhere in the rooms above.

Was there anybody up there?

Going to be noisy work, dismantling the duct pipe. But he had made noise already, and nobody had come to investigate; he had heard nothing to indicate occupancy. Have to go on the assumption that he was alone. No choice in the matter.

He would need tools to pry the flashing loose: the putty knife he had taken off the shelf, the tackhammer he had left there. He came back along the aisleway, and when he located the hammer he put it into the same pocket with the putty knife. As he turned again, the toe of his shoe nudged one of the apple crates—and it occurred to him that he would need something to stand on once he had cleared the duct opening. The top of the furnace was not high enough to let him reach all the way through the duct to move the register out of the way. And he would have to do that before there was anything for him to grab onto, any leverage to pull himself up.

He went over close to the furnace, bent, turned the candle to let melted wax drip onto the floor, and anchored it upright in the puddle. Got another candle out of the box, lit it, put it down nearby. They did not give off much combined light, but there was enough to throw the furnace and the duct pipe into dusky relief. Farther up, between the ceiling joists, the box flashing was concealed in heavy shadow.

Jackman squatted in front of an apple crate, tilted it, scraped apples out. Repeated the process with a second crate and then carried both of them around to the far side of the still. One at a time, he lifted them and slid them under the asbestos-wrapped hot-air piping and across the furnace top, out of the way. Now he had to get back there, between the water heater and the mash box and the back of the boiler. Copper coils, tubing, tin pipe, steel pipe—all interlocking and jumbling together like components in a Rube Goldberg invention. Wedge in past and through the piping, lean in, find purchase on the furnace edge. He banged his shin against a steel fitting, scraped the pulpy side of his head on one of the hot-air pipes, and clamped his teeth against the deep bites of pain.

Crouching slightly, he levered forward and up. Got a knee on top of the furnace, lunged and caught onto the base of the duct pipe and pulled the other leg up so that he was kneeling there head down, prayer fashion. He raised up alongside the duct, wrapped an arm around it and clung there while he groped for the hammer and putty knife, took them out and laid them inside the nearest of the two crates.

Off with the oils now: too bulky, restricting movement. He unbuttoned the slicker, shrugged out of it awkwardly, tossed it behind him and heard it flutter down in back of the still. Slid his knees around so that he was facing the duct pipe, hugged it with both arms and began to shove forward, pull back, in hard steady thrusts. The snap joint squeaked, bellied forth and back, loosened. Dry smell of dust. Jackman shoved again, wrenched back again, and when he felt the joint begin to separate he braced his weight against his heels and tugged less forcefully while still maintaining tension.

The pipe broke apart into two sections, screeching tinnily.

Dust sifted down, got into his nose and throat and made him cough. The ends of the two pieces of duct rested one on top of the other, off-center, canted up and down at opposing angles. He took his hands away and left the lengths like that and cocked his head, ears flared.

Stillness.

He reached up and ran his fingers across the nailed lips of the box flashing. Five nails in each, and all four lips solidly fitted to the wood crosspieces of the ceiling. He took the hammer and putty knife in his left hand, looped his right forearm over the hot-air run, bent one knee until his shoe was flat under him. Stood up, extending carefully, and found that he could stand fully erect; the top of his head just touched one of the joists.

Jackman transferred the putty knife to his right hand, felt out the flashing lip on the near side, and forced the squared blade between it and the ceiling. Worked it up and down, widening a tiny space as the nails began fractionally to loosen. But the blade was too thin, too pliable, to do any more

169

than that, and he switched the knife for the hammer and jimmied the claw end into the slit as far as it would go. Then he rocked it up, snapped it down hard.

Tearing sounds; one corner of the flashing popped free, and a nail dropped out and bounced metallically on the furnace top. The two pieces of duct pipe grated against each other as the upper section slipped outward. He nudged it with his thigh until he succeeded in dislodging it so that it hung free from where it was nailed into the flashing, no longer touching the lower section.

He moved the hammer claw over, wedged it tightly into the breach. Yanked downward again. The second lip came free, and the broken joint end jerked up and glanced off the hot-air run, and two more nails clattered at his feet. The section hung there now at a faintly vibratory angle.

Sweat stung the cuts and abrasions on the insides of his hands, and after he stooped to lay the hammer and the putty knife down, he dried them on the damp front of his sweater. Then he got a double hold on the flashing and twisted it up and down, side to side—facial muscles contorting into a wince at each thin squeal from the pulling nails. The left side gave first, and when it did the rest of the nails tore out one after the other, like the ripping of stitches, until the flashing and the section of duct came down severed in his hands.

He lowered it immediately, half-squatted to lay it on the furnace top and push it away toward the wall. When he rose up again, there was a sharp binding in his chest: breathing too rapid, too deep—starting to hyperventilate. He relaxed his jaws, opened his mouth and stood motionless, staring upward; the opening of the duct box was just visible in the guttering glow from the candles. No sounds filtered down through it from above, and there was only the faintest suggestion of gray light marking the position of the floor register.

While he waited for his respiration to shallow, he stretched both arms up and felt inside the opening. Smooth, dust-rimmed metal; no barrier against passage. He raised onto his

170

toes, but as he'd expected, he could not reach high enough to touch the register.

Bending again, he drew the first crate over and upended it, positioned it flush against the upthrust section of duct. Second crate bottom-up on top of it, angled slightly so that there was an open wedge on the lower crate to serve as a step. He raised his body, pressed down with his hands on the makeshift platform to satisfy himself that it was sturdy. All right—but he would have to keep his weight dead center to avoid slippage.

He put his right foot on the wedge-step, using the broken pipe and the hot-air run for balance. Brought his left knee up and anchored it on the second crate and then joined it with his right knee. Keeping one hand on the hot-air piping, he straightened from the waist and dug the fingers on his other hand into the joist alongside the duct opening.

Now the rough part: getting his feet under him. Draw the left knee up against his chest, toe scraping the crate slats, sliding forward until the leg was flat-footed. The crates wobbled under him, and he froze, sweat streaming down into his eyes. Inch forward then until the platform felt firm again. Position his head so that it was directly beneath the opening. And here we go, slow, slow, weight on the left foot, tendons protesting in arms and thighs and stomach; bring the right leg forward, toe skidding, heel coming down; both feet set . . . crates shifting again, slide the left foot back until they stabilized . . . and he felt his hair brush against one of the metal sides as his head pushed into the duct box.

He was not quite standing upright, but he would have to get his left arm inside before his shoulders. He took it away from the hot-air run, neck-bracing himself at the edge of the opening, and brought it up past his face and locked the elbow. The tips of his fingers pressed against the rough metal squares of the register, stiffened until he felt it shift and rise slightly inside the floor hole, and then relaxed again. Still holding onto the joist with his other hand, he straightened up full-length and pushed his shoulders inside the duct.

Going to be a tight fit. . . .

He spread the fingers against the grille, thumb back as far as he could extend it. Then, increasing pressure, he heaved up—and the register lifted out of the floor, and he was balancing it like a tray. The weight of it drove splinters of pain down his arm and into his armpit; dust burned in his nostrils, and he held his mouth clenched shut to keep from coughing and upsetting his precarious stance as he brought his arm and the register forward.

When he felt and heard the edge of the grille scrape against the floorboards, he eased his fingers back a square at a time and then shoved slowly, painstakingly. A third of the register cleared the opening, a half—

And it bound up on something.

Rug, he thought, goddamn rug. He got his fingers around the near edge and tilted it and shoved again. It would not move.

He wanted to scream with frustration, fought down the urge and pulled the register back, turned it diagonally and pushed again. It moved six inches, caught. You son of a bitch, you bastard thing—! He tilted it again, worked it across the edge of the floor opening to the far side, and started to push with violent jabs, and stopped himself in time and pushed steadily instead.

The register's right corner hung up again—but when he spun it around to the left it grated freely across bare wood. One last relentless effort, and he had it completely clear of the opening.

His left arm began to go numb from the strain, and he had to bring it back down past his face and take it out of the duct and let it hang loose at his side. He stood panting, drenched in oily, clammy wetness. I don't have enough strength left to pull myself out, he thought. All this way, all this struggle, and I can't get myself the hell up there.

Then he thought, angrily: Bullshit, that's defeatist bullshit. You can make it because you've *got* to make it.

Wait, rest awhile. Don't try it prematurely. Only going to

have one chance; once you kick free of the crates, you'll be committed: make it up or come crashing down and maybe break something.

Jackman flexed the fingers on the left hand, relaxed the grip of his right on the joist. Listen. Silence, except for the dry scratchiness of his breath. The jellied feel was back in his legs, some of the same numbness that was in his left arm, but he knew he did not dare move his feet on the crates. He began to count seconds silently to himself, still flexing the fingers. One minute. Two minutes. Three minutes.

I can't stand like this much longer. . . .

There was a tingling in his left arm now, and he was able to lift it from his side; the numbness evaporated into a series of dull throbbing aches. He put all his concentration on the arm, told himself he could feel strength seeping through it again and refused to believe that this was a lie. Strength in his right arm too, better take it down from the joist, better get it up inside the duct. Right arm first, that's the way to do it. Right arm up there tight on the floor, then the left.

He could make it now, if he was going to make it at all.

And he lowered the right arm and ducked down and brought it and the left arm inside the duct box, raised his body again. He could just get both forearms out of the opening above, palms flat on the floor on opposite sides. Then he shut his eyes, filled his lungs. Tensed.

Now.

He lunged upward off the crates, muscles contracting in his arms, legs kicking. There was a moment of loose suspension as his head came out of the floor hole; his calves scraped against the bottom of the duct box. Agony in his left shoulder and armpit, the arm going numb again, and he heaved frantically, flinging the arm outward along the floor; his fingers touched rough fiber—the rug—and dug into it, caught a handful of it just as he felt himself beginning to slide down. The rug did not give, it was weighted by heavy furniture, and it held him steady long enough so that he could twist to the right and get his ribcage jammed against

173

the edge, right forearm skidding across bare wood and onto the rug, that hand gripping it and pulling with it, and he was canted on his stomach for a second, and the next second it was his hip, and then he was half lying and half sitting on the rug with just his ankles stretched over the opening: out of the duct, out of the escapeproof locked cellar.

Out.

THERE WAS THE PALE GRAY oblong of a window in the rear wall, and just enough light coming through it to let him see the blurred outlines of a vanity table, a cedar chest, the corner of a headboard. Bedroom. Thin gusts of wind tugged at the weather stripping around the window, rattled a shutter somewhere at the front of the cottage. The other sounds were those of any old structure settling emptily in the cold hours of early morning.

His left arm was numb again, and he had to push awkwardly with the heel of his right hand to move himself backward with agonizing slowness until one shoulder butted against mattress and box springs. And he just sat there, wheezing hoarsely, because he knew he could not get up yet; even the desire for self-preservation could not make him get up yet. The effort in climbing out of the duct had been supreme, and it had wrung the last remnants of energy from him like droplets of water from a crumbling sponge.

And yet he felt totally controlled sitting there, as if with a kind of deliverance—as if the struggle to get free of the cellar had been an ultimate escape and horror could not touch him any longer. The undercurrent of fear was still with him, but it was submerged deeply in weariness and an existentialistic

174

resignation: he was not responding to it. He had been consumed, driven by terror for so long that he seemed to have developed a reactionary immunity to it, the way the body does to poisons administered in sustained, nonlethal doses.

He found himself thinking of Tracy as he waited. His feelings about her were a dull jumble in which only sorrow and pain were recognizable. If he had not brought her here to the island, she would still be alive. But if life and the universe were wholly ordered, if man was a wholly rational animal, there would be no wars and no apocalypses and he would not be where he was now. *If.* If you never crossed a street or walked a sidewalk, you could never be run down by a car. If you lived in hermitage on a mountaintop, you would not suffer from any of the evils of civilization. Where was the blame in anything that happened to you or to someone else in the normal course of existence? Where was the guilt? No man could be held accountable for circumstances beyond his control, for the whims of fate or a supposedly benevolent diety.

Rationalizations? Maybe. Maybe not.

I didn't know her, he thought. All the hours together, all the physical intimacies, and at the end of it we were still strangers. No love, nothing but sex and filmmaking. Interlude. A face in the night—the long night of a lifetime. What sense, what result except a crushing of self, in passively mourning the unjust deaths of strangers? All the strangers, like Alicia and the little boy in Saigon? *I'm sorry you're dead, I wish with all my heart that it didn't have to happen to you when it did, but it happens to all of us sooner or later. All of us. Sooner or later.*

The tightness in his chest lessened as the wheezing ceased, and the tingling sensation started up the left arm from wrist to shoulder. The fingers remained numb; when he lifted the arm experimentally, they hung like thick strips of flayed meat. He dropped them back onto the rug. More light seemed to be coming in through the window now, and he saw that the panes were misty. Close to dawn. Of what day?

Sunday, Monday? He had little perception of time, but except in terms of when the final moves would take place, time had ceased to matter.

Final moves, he thought.

Games.

And the realization came to him that throughout the ordeal in the cellar and the duct box, he had not once thought in terms of game-playing. Why? Every facet of his adult life had been translated into those terms, every action and reaction, every consideration; he had even managed to think of this nightmare as a game, foe against foe, move and countermove. But it was not a game—oh no, and it never had been a game.

Perhaps *nothing* was a game; perhaps the Old Man's philosophical legacy, like the Old Man's life, had been deceitful and fraudulent. And perhaps he had understood this subconsciously and had begun to reject game-playing, begun to exorcise finally and irrevocably, by extension, the Old Man himself.

That was an interesting insight, and he dwelt on it. The Old Man had dominated him during his lifetime, even dominated him from the grave; he had let himself be molded into the image of Thomas R. Jackman, so that in a spiritual sense the Old Man could live on one more generation in the son he had sired. Cheap, venal hunger for immortality. But hadn't the Old Man's entire life been predicated on a cheap, venal hunger for immortality? Hadn't that been the one true and absolute goal toward which he directed all his games—to leave an indelible mark on the pages of history?

Only he had failed, he had *lost*: he was already being forgotten, as liars and frauds—unless their sins were far greater and far more evil than his—were always eventually forgotten. Before long his mark would fade altogether, and his name would be nothing more than a meaningless word in political science books and moldering copies of *The Congressional Record*. The ultimate result of his game-playing had been death, nothing more, because if life was a game, then

176

death was the final outcome for all the players. You won the game of life by accepting its rules and living according to them; if you tried to cheat by dividing it up into private games of your own, with your own rules, you were a loser from the beginning.

Ironic how the change points in your life sometimes came about, how maybe they came about too late. And he *was* undergoing a metamorphosis, no mistake about that. He was in few ways the same David Jackman who had arrived on the island on Friday afternoon. Fear and horror and adversity and insight were the catalysts; you never saw yourself so clearly as when you were battling for the preservation of self.

Meg, Dale, the Old Man: he understood them all fully for the first time because he understood himself for the first time. Understood that the preoccupation with games which the Old Man had instilled in him had, more than anything else, been responsible for his slow and inexorable downhill slide toward a nervous breakdown and a personal destruction just as terrible in its own way as the one he faced here and now.

But before he could complete the rejection of the Old Man and of game-playing, and begin to reassess himself and his life, he had to survive; and survival meant winning this last deadly nongame.

He examined his feeling of resignation and found no apathy in it. He wanted to live, and he had not lost any of the rage and hatred, and he had the constant presence of pain as an added motivation. Friday night he had told Tracy that he could kill another human being if it meant saving his own life, and had not known then if he was speaking the truth; now he knew that he had been, knew too that he would do it without hesitation or compunction if it came down to that.

No more running and no more hiding, he thought.

Time to take a stand.

Always take the offensive whenever you can, David. Play with a certain amount of calculated recklessness, force your opponents off-guard; that's how you create vulnerability and that's how you win

177

your games. The Old Man had been right about that, so right. For all his charlatanism, Thomas R. Jackman had developed game-playing to a pseudoscience: if you wanted to win, you followed his advice to the letter.

So this one, this last one, is for you, Old Man, Jackman thought. The Final Moves of the Final Game, played in your honor, dedicated to your corrupt memory. You taught me how, you gave me the tools, and if I come out of it alive and intact I'll owe it all to you—and damn your soul for making me what I am.

His left hand began to tingle, then throb; he could feel the nap of the rug with the fingers. There were twinges in both legs, and a cramp in his right calf made him draw that leg up to flex it out. He sensed that he had enough strength finally to get up, and swung over against the bed, and got himself into a seated position on the quilt-covered mattress. The first time he tried to stand, the movement touched off a furious pounding in both temples, and a wave of dizziness forced him down again abruptly. He waited a minute or so, edged over to where a low nightstand sat beside the headboard, and leaned on that and tried again. The pounding was tolerable this time, the giddiness only transitory: he stayed upright, spreading his feet and stiffening his knees to keep them from buckling.

He was not ready yet to walk unaided, and he pressed in against the wall, and then took mincing steps around the nightstand and made it over to the window. The squall had moved inland to blow itself out, and it was no longer raining; the sky was a graying black, with a hint of a rose-colored flush above the tops of the trees eastward, and stars winked palely among tattered-lace clouds. In the half-light he could see drops of rain and dew glistening like tiny prisms on the fronds of a bed of lady ferns beneath the window. Gentling wind gusts provided the only movement.

As he stood there looking out, something nudged his mind, made him frown. Something wrong, something he was overlooking. Discordancy: he had felt it all along without be-

178

ing more than peripherally aware of it. But what? Moves? Rules?

His subconscious refused to give it up.

He put his back to the wall, and he was looking then at the closed sliding doors of a walk-in closet across the room. He took a step, wavered slightly and stopped, and took another: it was like walking on stilts, clumsy and teetering. But he got to the closet without falling, slid one of the doors open quietly, and looked inside.

Neat hanging rows of coats, dresses, shirts, slacks. He thought briefly of exchanging his own damp clothing for some of Jonas'—but Jonas was a small, wizened man, and none of his things would even come close to fitting. Still, the wet wool of the sweater chafed at his arms, and the clamminess of his shirt sent periodic chills along his back. Better to get out of those at least. There was a thick, folded blanket on the upper closet shelf, and he took that down and then stripped off the sweater and the shirt and draped the blanket shawllike around his shoulders, tied the ends into a double knot.

The closet contained nothing else of any use to him; he started out of the bedroom, hesitated, and went into the adjoining bathroom. The medicine cabinet yielded a bottle of aspirin and a package of cold tablets. He took out four of the aspirin and two of the tablets, clenched them in his palm, and came out and made his way up the hallway to the kitchen, supporting himself now and then on the walls.

The kitchen was large and old-fashioned—propane stove, porcelain sink set into a thick varnished-wood drainboard—and it had one window that looked out toward the main house, curtained in white chintz. He opened drawers until he found a long, thin carving knife; then he bent against the drainboard and peered out through the glass between the curtains.

In the distance the house had a hazy, gray appearance, insubstantial and weathered, as though it were little more than an abandoned shell. If there were any lights on inside, he

179

could not see them from this angle, and there was no outward glow on the waning darkness front or back. Most of the facing lawn was visible: they had taken down the charred cross, and they had removed the pole and its grisly crown. He did not let himself think of what they might have done with Tracy's head, or with her body.

When he was satisfied that the surrounding grounds were deserted, he drew back and opened one of the overhead cupboards and took down a glass. Ran a stream of cold water into it until it was full, swallowed the aspirin and the cold tablets one at a time. Forced himself to drink the rest of the water in small sips.

Hunger pangs made his stomach churn with faint nausea. How long since he had eaten anything? Didn't matter; he had to get something down now, something to help shore up his flagging strength. He put the glass on the drainboard and crossed in an old man's gait to the icebox. As he started to open it he thought of the light that might go on inside, and released the handle and stepped around instead to its side. He had to move it out slightly from the wall in order to expose the electrical cord and then hook the cord around his shoe and tug until the plug pulled free of the wall socket.

The icebox was only a quarter full: Jonas and his wife had probably taken perishables and a few other things with them to the mainland. But there was a small cantaloupe, and a container of homemade tomato juice, and a carton of eggs. Jackman took those out and put them on the drainboard, poured tomato juice into the glass and broke two eggs into it and blended the mixture with the knife blade. Then he sliced the cantaloupe in half, and one of the halves into slender sections, scraping out the seed pulp.

The juice went down all right, and stayed down, but he gagged on the first small swallow of cantaloupe. Had to spit it out into the sink to keep himself from vomiting. Wait awhile, he hold himself—and caught up the knife and took it with him into the hallway.

At the far end, to the right, was a utility porch with a washing machine and a dryer and a cement laundry tray on a wooden stand. Venetian blinds were partially drawn over the one window, but enough light filtered through to fade the darkness into gray-sheened shadows. He stepped to the back door and tested the knob. Locked. So they must have jimmied the lock on the front door and brought him in through there. When they came again, that would be the entrance they'd use—and that was where he would have to set himself up in ambush.

An idea came to him. There were storage cupboards on the wall and the side end of the porch, and two white-painted cabinets standing beneath them; he went there and opened each of the cupboards in turn. Detergents, a pile of rags. He bent to the cabinet on the left, and inside were an assortment of plumbing supplies, cans of touch-up paint and pipe dope and all-purpose oil, a plastic quart bottle of liquid drain-cleaner—

Drain-cleaner.

Jackman picked up the bottle, turned it over in his hands, but it was too dark for him to read any of the label. He set it on top of the second cabinet, opened the doors on that one. Wrenches, screwdrivers, a hammer, jars of assorted screws and fasteners, a hacksaw, a soldering iron, spools of wire solder. And what he had set out looking for: a spool of narrow-gauge, resilient copper wire.

Carrying the wire and the bottle of drain-cleaner, he returned to the kitchen and looked out again through the window at the main house. Dawn was breaking now, and the reddish tinge was brighter on the sky; the wind was dying. Nothing stirred anywhere that he could see.

He picked up one of the slices of cantaloupe, and this time he was able to swallow tiny bites without choking, without his stomach jumping. While he ate he read the label on the quart bottle, holding it up to catch the window light. As he had guessed, one of the ingredients was potassium hydroxide. All right.

When he had finished two of the slices and drunk a little

181

more tomato juice, he hunted through the cupboards until he discovered a widemouthed canning jar. He unscrewed the cap on the drain-cleaner and filled the jar to within an inch of the lip. Then, balancing the jar in one hand and the knife and the spool of wire in the other, he walked up the hall to the vestibule.

It was bare of furnishings, but on the right was the closed door of a coat closet. He reversed direction and entered the parlor that opened off to the south, just long enough to set the jar down on the nearest flat surface: Jonas' trestle desk. In the vestibule again he tried the front door, and it opened silently under his hand; he widened a narrow crack and put his eye to it and looked out. No one coming. And the fawn's head was gone from the porch, although he could see the dried smears of its blood at the door's edge.

He shut it again, moved over to the closet door and opened it all the way back so that the knob touched the wall. On the floor inside was a metal shoe rack fastened firmly to the back wall with screws. Jackman knelt in front of it on one knee, then unraveled two feet of the copper wire and looped the end around a crossbar near the bottom of the rack, six inches off the floor. Twisted the wire together in tight coils until it was secure, and he could not jerk it loose.

His legs felt wobbly again when he stood up, and he had to rest a shoulder against the jamb. Too much walking and too much added exertion; the nourishment he had taken had bolstered him a little, but he was still functioning on bare reserves. Not much more to do, he told himself. Get it done and then you can sit down and rest and begin the wait.

He pushed away from the jamb and backed up slowly, unwinding the wire. When he was standing in the entrance to the parlor, he checked the angle of the stretched length. Too far out from the door if he anchored it to something inside the parlor—more than five feet—because of the width of the outer partition separating the parlor from the vestibule. Where he wanted it was just beyond the full inward swing of the front door, maybe three feet.

Have to move out a piece of furniture, he thought; push it against the partition. No other way to do it.

Jackman turned to face into the parlor and scanned the room hurriedly. The horsehair sofa was too bulky, the straight-backed chairs too lightweight, the china cabinet too stolid. The desk? Yes: it was sturdy without being too heavy to move, and it was the closest object—he would not have to transport it far.

He put the knife and the spool of wire on the floor in the hall, out of the way. Entered the parlor and crossed to the curtained window in the side wall opposite the entranceway. The grounds outside were still deserted. He came back to the desk, transferred the jar to an end table, and cleared the polished top of blotter, inkwell, and a clutter of loose papers and miscellany. At the far side, then, he pressed the heels of his torn palms against the edge and thrust forward.

The carved wooden feet scraped loudly across the floor, but that could not be avoided. He gritted his teeth and kept on shoving, trying to ignore the muscle protest in arms and shoulders; the desk skidded out along the wall, into the entranceway. The knots in the blanket unwound and it slipped back off his shoulders, fell to the floor; he paid no attention. Got the desk turned and maneuvered it through into the vestibule and then, finally, a minute later, had it set solidly into the angle formed by the partition and the front wall.

Immediately he stumbled over to pick up the knife and the wire, came back with them, laid the knife on the desktop, and dropped to one knee again. Passed the spool around the pegged support piece just above the near foot, pulled the length taut, bound it with a dozen over-and-under loops. It seemed too close to the front door now. He struggled up and stepped over the wire and eased the door open, looked out. Solitude, bathed in a deepening reddish glow. Have to risk opening the door all the way, but do it fast—and he swung it in past his body, clinging to the knob. The edge rubbed against the wire.

Shut the door, return to the desk, drag it toward him eight

inches. Into the parlor. The jar of drain-cleaner, one of the straight-backed chairs; put the chair into the entranceway beside the desk, the jar down next to the knife.

And he was ready.

He caught up the blanket, wiped wetness from his face and eyes with it, redraped his torso, and lowered himself exhaustedly onto the chair, legs sprawled out in front of him. You can come any time now, he thought. Any time. Any time.

He waited.

AND WAITED.

And kept on waiting.

Light came into the vestibule from the two parlor windows, herding shadows down the hallway. The cottage was still. The air in there lost some of its coldness, became almost comfortable as the rising sun warmed the clapboards. Lassitude settled over him, and that and the effects of the cold capsules made him drowsy, blanked his mind for short periods so that he had to fight against torpor by constantly shifting position on the chair. His tailbone ached, his head ached, his hands ached—but all in a dull, tolerable way that did nothing to help keep him alert.

He got up once to stare out through the far window, saw nothing more or less than he had earlier. Came back and sat and waited. Got up again when his eyes drooped shut and had another futile look outside. Debated going to the kitchen for more tomato juice, decided against it, and sat down. And waited, waited, waited.

God*damn* it, why didn't they come?

The physical exertion of his preparations, then the lassitude, had blunted the nagging feeling of discordancy; but now it was bothering him again, gaining magnitude. It lay in his subconscious like a series of coded messages awaiting decyphering. Not unlike dreams, he thought then. Dreams, too, were coded messages. The Jabberwock dream in the cave. . . .

He stood once more, paced back to the parlor window. Concentrate. Messages. There was bright sunshine on the empty grounds, bright sunshine reflecting splinters of light off the glass panes on the house's near side wall, bright sunshine giving the blue waters of the bay a mercurial sheen. Midmorning now.

Messages.

Dreams.

Something overlooked, something wrong.

Discordancy—

Why hadn't they killed him as quickly as they had killed Tracy? Why had they left him alone in the dark cellar for so long? If they wanted to prolong the agony and the terror, why not have bound him, put him in a room with them and physically or at least mentally tortured him, let him watch them prepare for a blood rite while they watched him?

The sudden inpouring of questions, the breakthrough, the connection between conscious and subconscious turned him rigid and set his scalp to tingling. And immediately there were other questions, a chain of them: keys with which to decode the messages.

How had the Chris-Craft been stolen?

Why were the boathouse doors closed on Saturday morning?

How had they known he and Tracy would be on Eider Neck Friday night?

Why had they let Tracy and him escape through the marsh?

Why hadn't there been any axes and hatchets in the barn when he and Tracy went after the flare pistol?

185

How had they known he would be at the caves last night?

How had they known about the caves in the first place?

And as the messages decoded, as the answers became clear, Jackman felt a coldness settle like a hand between his shoulder blades. He reached into his trouser pockets, took everything out and stared at it. Two dimes and a quarter. Comb. Wallet. Key ring: keys for the house here, the house in Washington, his office, his car, his safe-deposit box. But that was all. That was *all*.

Proof.

When he had put the items away again, he stood looking blindly out of the window. He imagined a game board, the intricate design of a game board, all the pieces spread out along it; he saw the whole of the board, end to end, side to side, square to square—and each of the pieces took on form and clarity, each of the moves become recognizable. He studied it with his mental eye, fascinated, horrified. He had misinterpreted the rules all along: not just the moves, but the basic rules of the game.

Oh Jesus! he thought. Oh Jesus, Jesus, Jesus! Oh sweet Mary Mother of God!

He knew where their boat was.

He knew where the Jabberwocks were.

He knew exactly how he could win this Final Game.

Emotion swelled inside him, waves of it lifting, lifting, and when it crested the flood sent him hurrying back into the vestibule. His eyes glittered when he stared at the knife and the jar, over at the length of stretched copper wire. *Wrong move.* The strategy was not passive offense, it was aggressive offense. Take the game to them. Attack. Become the hunter instead of the hunted.

So the first moves toward checkmate, then, were ones calculated to confuse them and then separate them. Use one of the hidden game props they themselves had provided and used so successfully; turn the tables, hoist them on their own petard, divide them and conquer them—each of those clichés was applicable.

186

The lassitude was gone; he felt strong again, stronger than he had ever felt in his life. The rage and hatred were controlled, calculated, now. He threw off the blanket, took up the knife and the jar of drain cleaner from the desk, and ran down the hallway into the kitchen.

The same cupboard in which he had found the jar yielded a ring top and lid. He tightened those down to seal in the liquid. Opened drawers, found a cache of empty five-pound sugar sacks and put the jar and the knife, handle down, inside one of them.

He paused just long enough to swallow the last of the tomato juice; then he retraced his steps up the hallway to where a closed door on the right opened into a small sitting room. There was a shade drawn over the window in the facing wall, and he crossed to there and raised it. Outside were a hundred sunlit yards of grass, and beyond them the shadowed line of forest stretching from the headland to the interior of the island.

Jackman unlocked the window, lifted the sash, climbed over it, and used the cottage to screen the path of his staggered run for the trees.

DAPPLED WITH SILVERY HIGHLIGHTS, the sea licked placidly at the shale banks of the inlet on the headland's outer rim. Far out on the northeast, past Little Shad Island, a sailboat sat becalmed; it looked from this distance like a white handkerchief mounted on a stark blue background. Gulls dived in long elegant sweeps, cleaved the water neatly, and came up again trailing shimmery beads of spray.

Jackman stood resting for a moment beside the natural

rock bench near the edge, watching the gulls with eyes bright and resolute. Once into the woods he had slowed his pace to a rapid walk, to conserve energy, and his legs had held up amazingly well. Except for the asthmatic nonrhythm of his breathing, he did not feel weakened or otherwise affected by the trek across the headland.

He sat down on the rock, laid the sugar sack carefully beside him. And then he leaned forward and unlaced his shoes and took them off, took his socks off. Unbuckled his belt and unzipped his fly and stripped out of trousers and underpants.

He took the belt from its trouser loops, wrapped all the clothing and the pair of shoes into a tight bundle, and secured it with the belt. Standing, he brought his arm back and hurled the bundle discus-fashion into the sea. It made a heavy, audible splash when it struck, bobbed for a moment in the ripples, finally sank as the clothing became waterlogged. The surface smoothed again.

First and most important move completed.

Jackman looked down at his nakedness, and the thought came to him that he had reduced himself to primitivism. Naked savage, naked hunter. But the game itself was atavistic, and he was merely playing within its parameters, equalizing advantage. Naked, he had gained a momentary freedom—imperatively as well as symbolically.

Turning, he caught up the sugar sack and went back into the cool shade of the woods.

THE SUN WAS DIRECTLY OVERHEAD when he crept forward at the top of the rear slope, equidistant between the house and

Jonas' cottage, and lowered himself onto a grassy ledge dotted with wood asters. From there he could see over the cottage roof to the greensward across which he had run earlier, out along the full bayside curve of the headland. Most of the cove was visible straight ahead. All of it was empty, as motionless and vaguely illusory as a hologram. The high-noon stillness was acute; even the cries of the gulls seemed muted, like sounds emanating from somewhere outside the microcosm that the island had become.

He rested his chin on one forearm and eased himself into a more comfortable position, being careful of his exposed genitals. Rubbed the scratched and bruised soles of his feet against his ankles to clean them of pine needles and other bits and pieces of the forest floor. The sugar sack was within easy reach of his right hand; the tip of the carving knife protruded through the open end like a sharp metal tongue. For the first time he felt warm from head to foot: the day's heat had dried away the last lingering traces of dampness and chill. But his forehead and cheekbones were still feverish—the cold capsules and the aspirin seemed to have helped only a little—and he thought again, with clinical detachment, that he might have walking pneumonia.

The hell with it. The threat of pneumonia at this stage of things was meaningless. Unless it prevented him from functioning, and there did not seem to be any immediate danger of that.

He stared down toward the cottage. Nothing altered the fixed tableau. Once, after ten or fifteen minutes, there was a rustling in the undergrowth behind him; startled, he pulled the knife out of the sack and twisted over and sat up on one hip. A small gray squirrel darted out alongside a rotted stump and raced up the trunk of a spruce and disappeared among the boughs. Quiet resettled. He let himself relax, rolled over onto his stomach again and resumed his vigil.

When the man appeared and then came to a standstill at the front corner of the house, it was with such stealth that he seemed almost to have been there all along.

Jackman tensed but remained rigidly immobile. About time, sonny, he thought.

The sun glinted off the barrel of the rifle the man was holding at present-arms, put a glossy shine on the red-brown marks of the symbol painted on his bare chest. His hair was sandy, cropped short—the same color as his beard—and he might have been any age from twenty to thirty; he did not look as big in perspective as he had on Eider Neck, or last night on the cliffs, but then nothing looked the same as it had at those times. He stood for half a minute, moving his head in a slow 180-degree arc, and then he came out farther into the open space between the house and the cottage. No one followed him: he was alone.

Okay, Jackman thought. Okay.

The bearded man walked toward the front of the cottage, pausing now and then as though to listen. When he reached the end of the porch and started across to the steps, he vanished from sight.

Jackman held his position and kept his gaze steady on the cottage. Minutes trudged away in the silence. The glare of the sunlight seemed to intensify so that everything took on a lacquered, white-gold look, oddly surreal now; the sea shimmered with molten reflections.

And the bearded man appeared again, beyond the far front corner, moving in the same watchful fashion—but limping slightly now—at an angle toward the headland. Trip on the copper wire inside the door, did you, sonny? Too bad you didn't knock yourself senseless, you son of a bitch.

Wolfishly, Jackman's lips flattened in against his teeth. His eyes followed the man's progress across the rim of the beach, saw him stop once and turn a full slow circle. The deliberateness of his actions was that of a trained soldier. At the first of the trees on the long slope above the beach, he halted again and transcribed another small walking circle. Then he entered the woods, blended into the tree shadows.

When Jackman could no longer see him he got up with the

190

sack and went off in the opposite direction, laterally to the southwest.

HE MADE HIS RUN to the south wall of the house across exactly the same section of sloping ground that he and Tracy had covered in their rush for freedom the first night.

From behind the bole of a spruce he had studied the windows in that wall for several minutes before stepping out into the open, and he had seen no indication of a watcher; now, as he ran in a half-hobbled stride caused by the impact of his naked feet on grass-hidden rocks, he kept his head up and scanned the blind glass panes. Still no sign of anyone looking out. He came up at the wall just to the left of the storm doors, propped a shoulder against the clapboard siding, and listened. In the vacuumlike stillness, he thought, you ought to be able to hear sounds a long way off; he heard nothing.

They had closed the storm doors—he remembered that he had left them hinged open when he and Tracy burst out of the basement. He went over and caught the metal handle on one, tugged up. They hadn't bothered to replace the iron locking bars: the door half rose instantly under his hand. Exhaling through his nostrils, he dragged the door all the way up slowly to keep the hinges from squeaking, and laid it back. Sunlight cut into the gloom below, illuminated part of the wooden stairs. He paused to listen again—silence—and then stepped into the opening and started down, pulling the door half closed above him as he went.

When he was standing on the cold concrete floor, he waited to let his eyes adjust to the heavy black. Sunspots danced

191

at the periphery of his vision, fused into wavy distortional lines like those on an oscilloscope, then faded and vanished altogether. The darkness was absolute, and that meant the door to the pantry at the far end was closed. Otherwise, he would have been able to see some sort of light over there.

He felt his way forward until he was out of the annex. Vague shapes began to take form here and there, none directly in front of him. He recalled no obstructions in the path across to the inside staircase, but he had learned a wise lesson in Jonas' fruit cellar. Instead of trying to walk and maybe knocking over some unexpected object, he got down on his knees and began to crawl, holding the top of the sugar sack between his teeth. He had become very adept at crawling the past few days, he thought bitterly.

The cold floor, the dampness of the basement, robbed his body of sun-warmth and started him shivering again. His knees made faint slithery sounds on the smooth concrete. The outline of the steps loomed in front of him, and he got his right hand around the bottom of the railing support, took the sack in his left. Once he was on his feet again, he removed the knife from the sack, tightened his fingers around the handle, and rested that fist on the railing. Then he began the climb.

The third runner creaked sharply when he put his weight on it. He drew his foot back, froze.

The house did not lose any of its hush.

Jackman moved over to the side, located with his toes the end of the second runner where it was nailed to the frame, and tried again. No creak this time. He mounted the remaining treads in the same spots, soundlessly. Stood then on the narrow landing in front of the pantry door.

With the hand holding the knife he touched the knob, rotated it. There was a muffled click, and the door opened into the pantry on oiled hinges. Tensing, he used the knife point to push it perpendicular to the jamb. Retreated a half step instead of going forward and through into the pantry, and dipped into a slight crouch.

The shadowed larder was empty.

What he could see of the kitchen beyond was empty.

But he held his position, throat working dryly. A soft creaking came from somewhere in the center of the house. Natural grumbling of old timbers? Or someone moving around? He had no way of telling, not from here. And the sound was not repeated.

Step forward, into the doorway. Instinct told him the kitchen was as deserted as it appeared—but not the house. No, not the house. Inside the pantry he squatted and took the jar out of the sugar sack, gripped it between his right arm and chest, unscrewed the cap and lid carefully with his left hand and laid them on top of the sack. Cupped his palm under the bottom of the jar, fingers and thumb splayed upward around the heavy glass. Rising, he crossed to within one pace of the kitchen entrance.

Littered remnants of several lunches and dinners on the cobbler's-bench table: plates, glasses, utensils, an empty milk carton toppled on its side, orange peelings and apple cores and melon rinds. Rays of sunlight filtered in through the curtained window over the sink, extended dustily into the center corridor.

He entered the kitchen, walking on the balls of his feet, and went across it and stopped again just inside the right curve of the hallway arch. The air in there had a stifling warmth: they must have the furnace turned up to seventy or more. Like spiders, he thought. Flourishing on heat like a nest of spiders. There was silence in the hall, silence everywhere. He craned his head forward and began to ease it through the arch so that he could look up the length of the passage—

Bong!

Bong!

The sudden sounds erupted with the concussive volume of cannon shots, shredding the quiet and buffeting his sensitized eardrums like physical blows. He started violently and in reflex snapped his head and body back, and the move-

193

ment jerked his left arm up and out. Drain liquid sloshed over the mouth of the jar, splattered on the floor behind him. In automatic reaction he tightened his fingers and dug his nails into the glass to keep it balanced, to steady it; a droplet burned on one of the cuts in that palm. The surge of his heart swelled veins in both temples and set them to thudding. Clock, his mind said, goddamn bastard grandfather clock striking two P.M. He leaned shakily on the wall as the last echoes fled away, as the hush resettled to what seemed like an even deeper aphonic level than before.

The palm cut continued to burn hellishly, numbingly, as more liquid flowed down along the sides of the jar. He stood away from the wall and went over to the drainboard and took a dish towel off its cupboard hook. Put the knife and the jar down, not taking his eyes off the archway, and scrubbed at his palm and kept scrubbing at it until the fire diminished and the numbness disappeared. Then he dried the jar, set it once more into his cupped fingers, picked up the knife, and returned to the right curve of the arch.

From that angle he had to put his head only part way out before he could see the whole of the corridor. The bathroom, library and study doors were closed. Sunshine streaming into the parlor and through its hall entrance a few yards distant—but no other light of any kind—created in the duskiness a pale illuminated cube from floor to ceiling across the width of the hall; dust motes floated languidly inside.

Still moving on the balls of his feet, Jackman went to the opposite wall and sidestepped upward along its base. Part of the parlor came into view: sideboards, chairs, a third of the leather couch that faced the fireplace. Empty. He took three more steps, to the rim of the cube of sunlight.

Overhead and toward the front, a board creaked.

Again.

Jackman held himself still, not breathing. The creaking came a third time, and there was a short series of barely audible thumps. Heavy footsteps: the other man. He tried to

194

place the exact origin of the sounds, though they might have come from one of the forward rooms on the north side. His old room, or Dale's next to it. He waited, head tilted up, but he was listening to silence again.

He padded slowly across to the near edge of the entrance-way. With each step, more of the parlor appeared before him, and when he reached the edge and slid his back against it, one foot inside and one foot in the hall, he could see all of the room and through into the near half of the foyer. Unoccupied. And cheerless despite the sunlight, a part of him noticed—as though the violation of its genteel sanctity had destroyed all the summer memories and stilled forever the party laughter and the strains of music and the ghostly echo of the Old Man's voice.

He went the length of the parlor, glancing once toward the fireplace: the candles, burned down to blobs of yellowish wax, still remained on the mantelpiece and on the hearth, and the splashes and smears of dried blood still defaced the bricks like a madman's graffiti. But these things held no terror for him anymore; they only deepened his rage. When he took his eyes away from them, they no longer existed in the spaces of his mind.

A pace inside the foyer, he halted and looked over at the staircase. And a board creaked again above and beyond the top of the stairs, and he heard the same short series of heavy steps, louder now. He started to back away, then stood motionless when they ceased abruptly. Bedsprings protested as a weight dropped inertly and settled on them.

Quiet.

My room, all right, Jackman thought. My bed. Nice irony in that. Must have gone over to the window to look for the other one, and now he's come back to sit or lie and wait. Does he have the door open? If he's got the door open, he can see out into the hall from the bed.

Strategy. Up the stairs, take the chance the door is closed? No—the damned runners are liable to creak as loudly as those floorboards, and if the door *isn't* shut, there's no way to get to him without being seen first. Have to make him come out of there, then; make him come downstairs. Not too much time before the other one returns, it has to be fast. Knock something over, make some sort of noise? No good. That would only alert him, bring him down armed and prepared and blow the only advantage I've got. Has to be another way. But what? What?

He turned into the parlor again, stared searchingly around the room. Sweat rolled down his cheeks and dripped from his chin onto the sparse hairs on his chest; he did not bother to brush any of it away. His eyes quit their roaming, and he realized his gaze was fixed on one of the windows on the outside wall, on the bright flood of sunlight there.

Sunlight. Hot. Sweltering in here because of the sun and because—

The furnace.

But was there enough time before the bearded one came back? Calculated gamble; there was a risk factor in any move he made now. What you had to do was to choose the gambit that offered the least potential line of resistance in order to achieve optimum results. Wasn't that right, Old Man? Wasn't that the way you taught it to me?

There was only one thermostat in the house, and it regulated an even temperature throughout the upstairs and downstairs. It was here in the parlor, on the opposite wall by the center corridor. Jackman crossed to it, keeping his steps slow and measured. Set at seventy, as he'd guessed. He moved the dial full to the right, returned to the front wall and flattened himself there two strides from the foyer entrance.

One thing was certain: even if you thrived on heat, and even if you opened all the windows in one room, it would not take long before you started to suffocate when the day was this warm and the furnace was turned all the way up to ninety degrees.

AFTER FIVE MINUTES, the heat became uncomfortable.

After ten minutes, it became nearly intolerable.

Perspiration oiled Jackman's body, distorted his vision, fled in runnels down his naked torso and legs to create widening patches of wetness on the floor. Nausea kicked again in his stomach; his head drummed, felt light and giddy. The surfaces of his hands were slippery on the knife handle, on the mason jar, and he lowered three times to his haunches to dry the palms on an edge of the nearest rug.

At first the only sound from overhead had been a squeaking of springs as the man up there shifted position on the bed. Then his footfalls had thudded again, heavier, impatient or irritable or both, and there had been the scrape of the window sash being raised. Now, and for the past three or four minutes—utter silence.

Jackman kept expecting the front door to open, the other, bearded man to come stalking inside. It was like waiting for a slow-burning fuse to touch off a powder magazine: sooner or later, you knew it had to happen, and the longer it took, the more sure you were that it would be in the next second. Or the next. Or the next.

Waves of heat shimmered in the room, so thick and so intense they were palpable. Temperature had to be up into the eighties now. Breathing became painful, and his sinuses seemed to clog and swell. Dryness coated his mouth; dripping sweat filled the ridged cracks in both lips and needled there like bee stings. He squatted a fourth time to rub first one palm, then the other over the rough nap of the rug.

When he straightened, the footsteps began again.

This time they didn't stop within the confines of the room. This time they stumped away from the front of the house,

197

into the upstairs hallway—and there was no caution or suspicion in the quick, hard beat of them; there was only annoyance and discomfort. He was coming down, and he was not thinking about anything except the heat.

A rush of adrenaline made Jackman's heart beat concussively. He pushed back until he felt his buttocks flatten hard against the wall, raised the jar to neck height and held it out away from his body. The cords in his neck bulged like steel rods. Keep coming, keep coming! And the man was on the stairs, hurrying down the stairs with the same lack of suspicion, and Jackman heard him descend the last of the treads and pivot on the foyer floor, heard the congested plaint of his breath; then the Jabberwock started through into the parlor—quick perception of stubbled cheeks and dark hair, the faded image of the symbol on a bare chest, the butt of a handgun above his belt—and Jackman stepped out from the wall and hurled the contents of the jar, hurled the jar, straight into that hard young malignant face.

There was an instant of shocked comprehension before the drain-cleaner splashed into the staring eyes; the jar glanced off the man's chin, dropped away to one side. The sound of its impact with the floor was lost in a guttural scream. He flung his hands up to his face and reeled drunkenly into the parlor and struck an edge of the end table beside the sofa and knocked the lamp there to the floor, came staggering away in a graceless pirouette—all the while tearing animallike at his wounded eyes.

Jackman went after him and hit him in the small of the back with a lowered shoulder and sent him hurtling forward and into the bar in the far corner. One of the stools spun away and the other clattered into the outer wall, and the man dropped one hand blindly as he started to fall and caught the back edge of the bar, and his weight heaved it backward and then pulled it over and down across his legs as he jarred into the floor. Bottles and glasses shattered, bounced, rolled. The combined explosions of noise rattled the panes in the near window, reverberated hollowly on the heat-thick air.

The man struggled to unpin his legs, seemed then to re-member the gun in his belt and groped for it. But Jackman was down on one knee beside him by then, and he got his own hand on the weapon just as the other's fingers touched the butt, wrenched it free. Jabberwock made a frightened keening cry and swung wildly with both arms, like a groggy prizefighter; his eyes were swollen to sightless slits, streaked with tears and drain-cleaner, the skin around them blistered and flaming.

Pent-up hatred seethed through Jackman, twisted his mouth into a grimace. He started to raise the knife—plunge it down into that writhing chest, kill him, kill the Jabberwock. But the moaning cries grated in his ears, and he could smell the sour odor of the man's fear and pain, and the hand trem-bled and the muscles in his arm refused to unlock: he could not do it, he could not. Meaningless and cold-blooded act now. Aboriginal savagery, man reduced to his lowest com-mon denominator. When you stripped away the veneer of civilization, this was what you saw and this was what you were.

Jackman flung the knife viciously at the wall, sliding back away from more blind frantic swings, and took the gun by its barrel and slammed the butt into the side of the man's head. Grunt of pain, body spasms stilling into twitches; the arms dropped leadenly, and the cries became strangulated whimpers. Jackman tasted brassiness mingled with bile, steeled himself and drove the gun butt down a second time. The twitches and spasms ceased altogether. And the up-turned face, in repose, was eyeless—the face of a man out of the Dark Ages whose eyes had been plucked from their sock-ets and the wounds cauterized with a white-hot iron.

He lurched to his feet, looking away, and dry-retched. Then he stumbled into the foyer and paused beside the door to regain control of his breathing, to search for sounds from outside. There were none. He cracked the door, peered out at the beach, across the veranda at the headland and the front of Jonas' cottage. Sun-washed desertion. Momentary relief pulled a sigh from him; he closed the door and ran back across the parlor.

The waves of heat battered at his body, and he veered to the thermostat and spun the dial back to sixty. Leave it up the way it had been and eventually the furnace would blow. Then he knelt again beside the unconscious man, not looking at the distended face, and began to fumble through the pockets of the Levi's he was wearing.

Luck was riding with Jackman now: he found what looked like a boat key on a metal ring.

Now he could get off the island. *Now* at long bloody last.

Checkmate—almost.

Standing, clenching the key in moist fingers, he hesitated. Take the pants too? Time, time. But he would need to wear something when he came in to Weymouth Village, and this one was about his own size; they would fit all right. He made his decision: set the gun and the key down and opened the belt with both hands, opened the Levi's and unzippered them. Glanced furtively over his shoulder, still expecting the front door to burst inward at any second, and then tugged the jeans over the shoes and got them off. Stood up quickly and stepped into them, fastened the button at the top but left the belt ends hanging. Then, gun in one hand, key in the other, he ran once more into the foyer. Listened, eased the door open.

Stillness.

Luck holding, holding.

Jackman retained a breath, threw the door wide and came out running. Down the porch steps, across the lawn, onto the path that skirted the edge of the cobble beach. His bare feet slapped against the packed earth; the hard glare of the sun dried the oily sweat on his back and face. He swiveled his gaze from the tip of the headland around to the cottage, saw nothing except an unbroken wall of trees, a motionless sweep of grass.

His destination was the dock; he raced out along it, came up hard against the closed boathouse door and fumbled at

200

the knob. Turned it and pulled the door open and stepped inside, closed the door behind him. He stood for a moment in the semidarkness, blinking.

When his eyes adjusted he saw the Jabberwock's boat—a fifteen-foot inboard-outboard—tied to the left-hand walk.

But it was not alone in there: the Chris-Craft, undamaged, was moored opposite.

Jackman was not surprised; he had expected to find both boats. So damned obvious all along, like the purloined letter in the Poe story. He swung down into the inboard-outboard, fitted the key into the dashboard ignition. It was the right one; it slid easily into the slot, and when he turned it the lights in the gasoline gauge and the tachometer came on.

He left the key in the ignition, climbed out onto the walkway, and went to where the long hooked pole lay near the outer doors. Tucked the Jabberwock's gun into the waistband of the Levi's, bent to pick up the pole. Started to turn toward the outer doors.

And the dockside door burst open suddenly and the bearded one, rifle balanced in the crook of one arm, stood framed against the brassy rectangle of sunlight.

THERE WAS AN INSTANT of frozen shock, and the thought came to Jackman that the bearded man must have been up in the perimeter of the trees, must have seen him make his run from the house; but even while he was thinking that, the momentary paralysis left him and a fresh surge of fury made his reaction immediate and instinctive. He was beyond capitulation, beyond retreat; the gamesman in him was wholly geared to attacking.

201

He took a firmer grip on the pole, sliding his right hand back on the shaft, planting his left foot, the one pointing toward the Jabberwock. When the bearded man saw him moving he started to snap the rifle out and up, to bring the weapon to bear. Jackman put all his weight on the left foot, pivoted forward.

And hurled the pole like a trackman throwing a javelin.

The bearded man was still partially blinded by the sudden change from glaring light to semigloom, and he did not seem to see the pole until after it left Jackman's hand and came flying toward him; he dodged sharply to his right, half turning, staggering off-balance. The pole just missed his head, sailed past him and out through the open door, clattered on the dock and then skidded off into the bay.

Jackman had started running as soon as he released the pole, fumbling the handgun out of his waistband; but he had no intention of firing it, he had never fired a gun in his life, he thought of it only as a club. He came in on the bearded man before the other could regain his equilibrium, and his wrist and the side of the pistol cracked across the Jabberwock's neck, spun him backward and hard into the wall beside the door. The bearded man made a growling noise, twisted and slashed out with the rifle barrel, and the front sights gouged into Jackman's ribs.

Flare of agony: he gasped and a red mist wheeled behind his eyes. He groped for the rifle and managed to catch hold of it with his free hand and get a fisted grip on the barrel, turning his body on blind impulse away from the muzzle. But the bearded man was stronger, unhurt, and he ripped the rifle free and the sudden movement laid the barrel up on his shoulder, baseball fashion, Jabberwock at the Bat, and he tensed to swing it as he or the one in the house had swung the board last night on the cliffs.

In defensive fury, wielding the handgun, Jackman plunged into him, and there was a moist slapping sound when their chests came together. The rifle barrel cleaved air harmlessly past Jackman's shoulder, but then struck a glancing blow on his right forearm; the pistol slipped out of sweat-slick fingers, bounced on the walkway behind them. Jackman heaved up in reflex, under the rifle, and the impact tore it loose, sent it clattering after the pistol; small dull echoes fled through the enclosure.

Jabberwock's fingers dug into the muscles across Jackman's back, wrenched him around. They staggered sideways into the doorway, scraped off the jamb and reeled out onto the dock like a pair of stumble-footed dancers. Jackman kicked at an ankle, felt the heel of his foot strike bone: the bearded man grunted and lurched hard forward, off-balance again. Jackman's sole slid across the edge of the dock, into empty space, and he felt himself toppling over backward, falling with a sickening sensation of weightlessness—and both of them, locked together, plunged down into the crystallike surface of the bay.

Sheets of water mushroomed up around them, consumed them and poured into Jackman's open mouth, into his nose; the icy shock of it constricted his lungs. They tumbled over in a kind of aquatic somersault so that the bearded man was above when the roll ended and their momentum ceased. Through the swirls of white froth, Jackman could see the staring eyes and the distorted face close to his own, as ghastly in the murky light as that of a sea creature. Arms like tentacles slithered over his bare torso, fingers scratched and fumbled at his throat.

He thrashed frantically, parrying, trying to get his legs under him so that he could lunge upward; but weakness and the absence of oxygen made the movements sluggish. Pressure built to a roaring inside his head, seemed to expand it until it felt enormous, ready to burst. Panic assailed him again for the first time since his escape from the fruit cellar.

Air!

One of the grasping hands caught his jaw, hung on with nails gouging. He twisted his neck in a forward quadrant, broke the grip and felt his cheek touch the inside of the bearded man's forearm. Flailed up with his elbow, and there was a solid impact—got him across the breastbone—and the man rolled aside. Desperation gave Jackman the power to pull his legs in, kick them out scissoring, and claw himself upward at an angle like someone climbing a ladder. Fingertips grazed his ankle, slid away—

Air!

—and his head broke surface and he shook it and opened his mouth and made a sucking, gasping noise. His chest heaved and then there was a burning pain and his lungs inflated, deflated with a spitting whoosh, inflated again. Salt blurred his vision, but he could see that he had come up directly in front of one of the dock pilings, near where the hooked pole—too light and porous to sink—bobbed on the disturbed surface. He looked wildly toward the beach: too far away, he could not swim fast enough to get clear. Looked back and saw the pole, the pole, and threw out an arm and his fingers closed around it below the metal hook.

Three feet to his left, Jabberwock's head surfaced. And the upper half of the man's body hurtled out of the water in almost the same motion, seallike, eclipsing the sun at the apex of his lunge.

Jackman had just enough time to drag the pole diagonally across the front of his body, lean back and get the metal hook up like a spearhead before his face.

The bearded man saw the pole and the hook at the last second, tried to wrench away from it—too late. The knobby upper end of the hook caught him just above the bridge of the nose with an audible cracking thud.

Jabberwock went rigid, became a sudden inert weight, and his body drove Jackman under again, drove the pole out of his grasp and down and away from him. He had managed to retain a breath, to get his mouth clamped shut so that no water spilled in; he twisted aside from the weight, pulled his legs under him—and felt the soles of his feet scrape over the rocky bottom just before he kicked upward and through into daylight again. Shallow water, shallow enough for him to stand. And thank God for that: he did not have enough strength left to swim more than a few strokes.

Panting thickly, anchoring the balls of both feet to keep his head clear of the water, Jackman stared over at where the bearded man had gone under. A moment later Jabberwock's naked back appeared in a loose, face-down float. The head did not lift or turn; the body did not move.

Jackman waited—but no one could hold his breath that long, or float with that stillness if he was conscious. Finally he took half a dozen bobbing steps to the other man and slapped weakly at the head with his palm: It wobbled, did not come up. He hoisted it out of the water by the hair, turned it, and the eyes were closed, the mouth contorted into a rictus of pain. There was a pulpy-looking indentation above the nose, where the hook end had struck; ruptured blood vessels beneath the skin stained it with spreading blue-black color.

Dead, Jackman thought. Or was he? Didn't the eyes of a dead man come open and his features go slack?

He rolled the bearded man onto his back, lifted one of the limp arms and felt for a pulse. It was there, faint and irregular. Concussion, then—maybe a skull fracture. It would be a long while before he came around again.

Checkmate.

Tension drained out of Jackman, left him limp and a little dizzy. The Final Game was over now, indisputably finished.

O frabjous day! Callooh, callay. . . .

He was kneeling on the sun-hot cobbles of the beach, head hanging down, and there was little strength left in his arms.

205

When he raised his head he saw the Jabberwock lying on his back in a nest of seaweed at the water's edge. Jackman vaguely remembered thinking that he couldn't leave the bearded man out in the bay to drown, and then grabbing a handful of the sandy hair, but he could not recall anything about the swim in to the beach. Lost time, timeless time.

He knelt there for a while longer, until he was sure he could move without collapsing. Then he crawled to the bearded man and turned him over with hands that were alternately steady and paroxysmal, opened his belt and pulled it out of the trouser loops. Kneed the body prone again, dragged the arms back and belted them together.

When he searched the pockets he did not find anything at all.

Jackman managed to stand with effort, made his way across the beach and across the path to the nearest of the ornate iron lantern poles jutting out of the lawn. He leaned against it, staring up at the house. The sun's rays dried him, lay across his back like a healing hand; strength flowed back into him slowly. He heard the screaming of seabirds with an acute suddenness that made him realize he had not been hearing anything at all for several minutes.

And something seemed to make a soft creaking sound a long way off, and he turned his head but could not locate the sound. There was not a breath of wind, and the sun-glare was so intense that it created mirages and false shadows. Nothing that could have made the creaking sound. Trick of the mind—?

Soft creaks, he thought.

Yes.

He started walking again, up the slope to the veranda, up the steps to the front door. It stood ajar; he pushed it wide and entered the foyer. It was still oppressively hot in there, but the palpable waves of heat were gone. Through the parlor arch he could see the still form of the first Jabberwock lying in exactly the same position as before, half pinned under the toppled bar.

Jackman turned for the stairs, mounted them deliberately, looked into his old room. Then he pushed open the door to Dale's room, the door to one of the guest rooms. The door to the master bedroom was already standing wide; he went up to it and stared inside.

And kept on staring, leaning against the jamb.

"Hello, Ty," he said, and watched Tracy—the third Jabberwock—get up off the antique four-poster and stand stiffly facing him.

SHE WORE A PAIR of slacks and a scoop-neck blouse, and her hair was freshly washed, freshly brushed. Artfully applied makeup covered the healing scratches on her cheeks. She looked young and soft—except for her face. It was an emotionless mask, full of age, and the eyes were as empty as abandoned, half-finished houses.

Jackman felt nothing at all, looking at her. No surprise, because he had known for hours that she was alive and might still be on the island; because the soft creaks he had seemed to hear outside were in reality echoes in his memory: those he'd heard when he came up naked through the basement earlier, soft creaks at the center of the house when the Jabberwock's steps had been heavy in Jackman's old room. Nor was there any of the rage, the hatred that he had focused on the other two. He was bereft of emotion; the fight with the one at the boathouse had left him hollow, at least for a while. And maybe that was something to be grateful for.

"I've been waiting for you," Tracy said, and her voice was as empty as her eyes. "It was obvious you'd guessed the truth when the transmitters stopped working properly, and I

207

thought you might come after what happened downstairs. When you didn't, I went down and opened the door and saw the whole thing at the boathouse; I knew you'd come then."

"Why didn't you run and hide?"

"Why should I? I might as well face you now as later."

He came into the room and leaned heavily against the dresser. A feeling of detachment had begun to seep through him. "Transmitters," he said. "Let's see: a crystal-controlled voice transmitter, and some sort of homing bleeper. Sophisticated, long-range, waterproofed. Right? I've read enough reports on electronic surveillance; I should have tumbled long before I did."

She was silent.

"Where were they hidden?" he said.

"You didn't find them?"

"No. I might have if I'd looked for them, but just knowing they existed was enough."

"The voice transmitter was in your belt buckle," she said tonelessly. "The other one was in a shoe heel."

He nodded. "The outfit you gave me before we left Washington."

"Yes. So that was how you guessed the truth—the bugs."

"Partly. It was the only explanation for those two always knowing where we were and where I was—Eider Neck, the barn, the cliffs last night. And it was the only way they could have known about the caves: I had to have told them myself, through conversation with you."

"What else gave it away?"

"The Chris-Craft being stolen, for one. It's not nearly as simple to cross ignition wires on a boat as it is on a car. So it followed they might have had a key, and the only way they could have gotten one was if you'd taken *my* key while I was sleeping Friday night and passed it over. I knew that was the answer when I checked my pockets this morning and didn't find the boat key.

"Then there was the missing axes and hatchets in the barn when we went for the flare pistol. Those things were there

Friday night; I saw them hanging on the wall. But all the knives and cleavers had been left here, in the kitchen, so they couldn't have been worried I'd use an ax or a hatchet as a weapon. Which left one answer: I wasn't supposed to escape the barn easily or too soon, because all of you needed time to stage the fake murder and set up the fake severed head and the animal blood.

"I was expected to believe you'd been killed quickly, but when they got me last night all they did was lock me in the cottage cellar. Didn't make sense unless they had no intention of murdering me at all, unless they figured to accomplish their real purpose by leaving me alone there."

He stopped speaking; the words were thick and bitter on his tongue, and he felt he had been talking as if by rote. But he was thinking of the Jabberwock dream, and the subconscious message that Jabberwocks were nothing more than the creations, like things that went wobble-wobble on the walls of the mind, of a nineteenth-century fantasy writer—mythical creatures living in mythical lands and presenting illusory menaces. Of Charlie Pepper, who had taught him about old Mr. Bugbear, and that there was never any reason to be afraid of what you don't know or what you don't understand or what you only think might be. And of the Old Man, from whom he had learned all there was to know about game-playing.

He did not tell her any of these things, because she would not have understood.

She stood motionless, and after a time she gave a short, mirthless little laugh. "Funny," she said. "I thought it was such an airtight scenario—the best thing I'd ever written."

"Oh it was good, clever," he said. "A game that wasn't a game that *was* a game. A murder that wasn't a murder, a head that wasn't a head. Illusion, misdirection, moves within moves. Careful manipulation too: let me make all the decisions, anticipate my reactions, guide me through the prescribed moves."

She was silent again.

"What I want to know now is who produced it? Not those other two; they're pawns, set pieces like you and all the rest of it."

Imperceptible shrug. "Alan Pennix."

That did not surprise him; nothing anyone did or said would surprise him for a long time. He said only, "Why?"

"Your politics, for one thing."

"That's not enough, even for a man like Pennix."

"There was a girl—he says he loved her."

"Alicia?"

"Alicia. Trite, isn't it?"

He knew what was coming. "She committed suicide, didn't she?" he said.

"Yes. In a town down south somewhere last September. Just before she did it, she called Pennix and told him; he couldn't talk her out of it. She blamed you."

Jackman winced. But he was no longer able to accept that burden of guilt any more than he had been able to accept guilt when he believed Tracy to be dead. It belonged not to him but to the being that had been Alicia, and to the fates that controlled the universe.

He said, "Why this elaborate plot for revenge? Why not something simple, something out of Nixon's bag of tricks maybe?"

"It didn't start out to be elaborate. But Pennix wanted you to suffer. He knew you had emotional problems; he found out somehow that you'd spent two weeks in a private hospital last year."

"And he thought I could be broken."

"Yes."

"So he hired you to get next to me, to set something up."

"Yes."

"Did you really need six months to find a way?"

A shadow passed across her face, vanished again. "There were other opportunities," she said. "But he didn't like any of them. He's a patient man."

And a venal one, Jackman thought. Just like the Old Man.

He said, "Why you?"

"I was balling him—I still am, if that matters—and he bared his soul to me one night. That's all."

"How much did he pay you?"

"I didn't do it for money."

"Then it was just a game to you, is that it?"

"Does that disgust you?"

Yes, he thought. All games disgust me now. "Isn't there anything that touches you, Ty?" he said. "Isn't there anything you care about?"

The shadow came again. "Would you believe me if I said I cared about you as much as I could ever care about anyone? That it was partly my doing Pennix didn't act on any of those other opportunities? That I almost didn't go through with it this weekend, and that I'm not so sorry it turned out the way it has?"

Jackman stared at her.

"No," she said, "I didn't suppose you would. But then, it doesn't matter, does it? It's too late now." Her mouth tightened. "All right, you want to know why I did it? I did it because I live for just one thing, the only thing worth living for. Orgasm. I told you that Friday night. And this was the biggest turn-on of my life; it was something to get off on for *months*, do you understand? Unrelieved ecstasy."

He turned abruptly away from the dresser, went to the doorway on legs that felt swollen and heavy.

Behind him she said, "What are you going to do when you get back to the mainland?" but not as if she really cared.

"To you? Nothing. I don't want revenge; that's for fools like Pennix. All I want is for you to get everything cleaned up out here before Jonas comes back tomorrow—the blood, the props, all of it. That's the way it was supposed to work anyway, wasn't it? No telltale signs to corroborate a madman's story. Just the madman and his mad tale."

Silence.

He looked at her for the last time. "Where's the key to the Chris-Craft? It wasn't on either of the other two."

"In your old room. On the desk."

He turned again.

"Good-bye, David," she said.

Jackman went out without answering, leaving her there alone with her words and her thoughts and her emptiness.

EPILOGUE

Monday Afternoon, May 25: THE ISLAND

Out of life's school of war: *What does not destroy me, makes me stronger.*

—NIETZSCHE, *Twilight of the Idols*

THE STARK WHITE GLARE of the sun had begun to fade slightly when Jackman came outside, and sharp-edged afternoon shadows were gathering in the island forests. Against the too-blue backdrop of the sky, the tree boughs had a sooty, wilted look. The resin smell, the ocean smell, seemed tainted with the overriding odor of dust and heat.

He walked slowly down to the dock. The man on the beach had not moved, and the sun had baked his naked back to a brick-red color. Far off to the south, a speedboat made figure-eight loops on the smooth face of the sea, trailing plumes of spray. The screeching of the gulls grated in his ears, scraped at nerve ends like fingernails drawn across a blackboard.

When he entered the boathouse he saw the rifle and the handgun lying where they had fallen during the struggle earlier. He picked them up, carried them onto the dock, and threw them one by one into the bay. Then he went back inside and used an emergency oar from the Chris-Craft to open the outer doors. Untied the cruiser's bow and stern lines and stepped down behind the wheel.

For a time he sat limp, resting, in the helmsman's chair. He thought briefly of Tracy, but she was as unfathomable to him as a beautifully carved idol from a culture far removed from his own. Forget her. And forget Alicia. The future was all that mattered now; the past was dead and awaiting burial, and so was the David Jackman who had lived it.

Meg? Well, Meg was part of that dead past. A loveless marriage, a marriage of convenience, had no place in a new beginning. When he got home to Washington, to their red-brick Georgian house in Georgetown, he would have to sit her down and tell her he was ending it.

Pennix? Confront him eventually, make it clear to him that any future attempts at mindless vengeance would result in criminal charges and public exposure. And then make him pay for this weekend in the only way it counted: in the political arena.

Himself, his career? He did not know yet whether he would continue in politics, learn to be a better senator as well as a better man—or finish out his term and then attempt twenty years late to pursue the dreams of his college years, the promise of *I, Camera, Eye*. Time would determine the choice, and make it the right one; time would determine everything.

He roused himself at length and started the cruiser's engine. Backed the boat out into the bay and swung it in a tight arc and took it out toward the breakwater at quarter throttle.

When he passed the tip of Eider Neck he looked back at the house, the cottage, the barn—and saw them now through different eyes, in a wholly different perspective. They were no longer the intimate, beckoning monuments of the sweet (but not so sweet) summers of his youth; instead there was about them an atmosphere of subtle decay, of false and grotesque nostalgia, like mausoleums in an old pastoral graveyard. The silhouetted forestland and the long grassy hump of the Neck and the broad flat sea and the ascendant land that marked the cliffs seemed alien to him: he felt no communion with them now, no sense of need or love or joy, no

216

sense of a good high place on which a man could stand and perhaps learn to touch infinity.

This was Jackman Island, nothing more, and the Jackman to which it had belonged from the beginning was the Old Man—in the flesh and in the spirit. It was never mine, he thought; I never possessed any of it. Once, he might have claimed it for his own, but that time was long gone, had been forfeited through weakness and self-delusion. When he had discovered himself, he had lost the island forever: he could never return to it again.

He put his back to it and pointed the cruiser toward the eye of the westering sun.